BREAK
WATER

BREAK WATER

BOOK 2

THE ELEMENTAL SERIES

SHANNON MAYER

USA TODAY BESTSELLING AUTHOR OF *RECURVE*

Breakwater (The Elemental Series, Book 2)
Copyright © Shannon Mayer 2015
Copyright © HiJinks Ink Publishing, Ltd. 2015

All rights reserved Published by HiJinks Ink LTD.
www.shannonmayer.com

All rights reserved. Without limiting the rights under copyright reserved above, no part of this publication may be reproduced, stored in or introduced into a database and retrieval system or transmitted in any form or any means (electronic, mechanical, photocopying or otherwise) without the prior written permission of both the owner of the copyright and the above publishers. Please do not participate in or encourage the piracy of copyrighted materials in violation of the author's rights. Purchase only authorized editions.

This is a work of fiction. Names, characters, places and incidents are either the product of the author's imagination or are used fictitiously, and any resemblance to actual persons living or dead, business establishments, events or locales is entirely coincidental. Or deliberately on purpose, depending on whether or not you have been nice to the author.

Original illustrations by Damonza.com

Mayer, Shannon

Acknowledgments

As always, I have to thank my amazing support group who stand by me when I feel like I'm losing my mind, fighting to get characters to behave or even just need someone to tell me that yes, I can get this book written too. My editors Tina Winograd (and assistant), N.L "Jinxie" Gervasio, beta readers Lysa and Creig Lessieur, and Jean Faganello (aka Mom) have helped to make this book shine under their gentle (and sometimes brutal) edits. :) Honestly, I couldn't ask for a better crew to help me out with my writing. Of course, my readers have to be mentioned too, because without their enthusiastic embracing of Larkspur and her adventure in "Recurve", I don't think "Breakwater" would have come to life the way it did.

Last but not least, to the two men in my life. One tall and handsome, one tiny and handsome. You two are the reason I get up at the crack of dawn, and stay up past midnight to make these books happen. You are my motivation, and the reward I have for doing what I love.

ALSO BY SHANNON MAYER

THE RYLEE ADAMSON NOVELS

Priceless (A Rylee Adamson Novel, Book 1)
Immune (A Rylee Adamson Novel, Book 2)
Raising Innocence (A Rylee Adamson Novel Book 3)
Shadowed Threads (A Rylee Adamson Novel, Book 4)
Blind Salvage (A Rylee Adamson Novel, Book 5)
Tracker (A Rylee Adamson Novel, Book 6)
Veiled Threat (A Rylee Adamson Novel, Book 7)
Wounded (A Rylee Adamson Novel, Book 8)
Rising Darkness (A Rylee Adamson Novel, Book 9)
Alex (A Rylee Adamson Short Story)
Tracking Magic (A Rylee Adamson Novella, 0.25)
Elementally Priceless (A Rylee Adamson Novella 0.5)
Guardian (A Rylee Adamson Novella 6.5)
Stitched (A Rylee Adamson Novella 8.5)

THE ELEMENTAL SERIES

Recurve (The Elemental Series, Book 1)
Breakwater (The Elemental Series, Book 2)

PARANORMAL ROMANTIC SUSPENSE

The Nevermore Trilogy
Sundered (The Nevermore Trilogy, Book 1)
Bound (The Nevermore Trilogy, Book 2)
Dauntless (The Nevermore Trilogy, Book 3)

URBAN FANTASY

A Celtic Legacy Trilogy
Dark Waters (A Celtic Legacy, Book 1)
Dark Isle (A Celtic Legacy, Book 2)
Dark Fae (A Celtic Legacy, Book 3)

THE RISK SERIES
(WRITTEN AS S.J. MAYER)

High Risk Love (The Risk Series, Book 1)

CONTEMPORARY ROMANCES
(WRITTEN AS S.J. MAYER)

Of The Heart

Chapter 1

The ocean lapped around my feet, tickling my toes, and for a moment I forgot why I was there, the peace and comfort was so strong. The mother goddess stood over me, her image shimmering as if she were within a heat wave. Her long skirt trailed behind her in the air, dancing on currents I couldn't see. Deep brown hair like the richest soil of the earth with hints of silver glinted in the sunlight. Green and gold eyes sparkled with what I could only target as mischief. "Child, the bonds Cassava placed on your soul are deep and well-rooted. I can begin their undoing, but you must be the one to finish it."

She directed me to lay down, her hands gentle as she guided me. Flat on my back, I dug my fingers into the wet sand under me. "How long do I have to complete the breaking?"

"Once I begin, you will have time. But . . ." *She held a hand over me, and through her fingers I saw all five colors of the* elements swirl. Green, blue, red, white, and pale pink. Earth. Water. Fire. Air. Spirit.

"But what?"

Her softly swaying hand mesmerized me more than a little, like a cobra with a tiny mouse. The analogy perhaps wasn't so far off base. She leaned toward me, her eyes a deep, glowing green and gold.

"Be warned. The power that resides in you is that of ten elementals. Your mother's bloodline has done that for you, charging your abilities and connection to the earth beyond that of any elemental who walks this world. You may not understand now, but you will one day. Be patient, child of mine. Your time will come."

"Before you start, what about my father? Will he not need to be broken apart too? Cassava was as much in his mind as she was in mine."

The mother goddess smiled, but her mouth was not kind. "Basileus was older when Cassava worked Spirit on him. His mind already formed. His journey back is different from yours, Larkspur, and you cannot hurry it along."

She lowered her hand until it hovered over my feet. The five colors shifted, spinning faster between her fingertips. At first, her touch was cool, her skin soft and smooth; safe, I was safe with her.

With a speed I couldn't follow, heat radiated from her hand. The water around my feet bubbled and foamed. I wanted to scramble away, out of the water, farther up the shoreline.

But I couldn't move, my body seemingly frozen to the ground. A moan slipped out of me as the heat escalated, chased by my fear I was about to be cooked alive.

"This will not be pleasant, Larkspur."

Jaw tight, I didn't answer, just tried to breathe through the fear climbing my body like a monkey shimmying up a tree, screeching once it reached the top. The sizzle and crackle of my skin rose to me as the water heated past boiling. Her touch held me down. Moans turned into screams as the heat exploded up my legs, bursting through my bones, shattering my body into tiny molecular elements.

"Soon, child, it will be done soon."

A wave of water washed over me, dousing the heat and leaving me blessedly chilled to the core. The water didn't recede, though. It clung to me, smothering me. I wanted to thrash against the bonds the mother goddess placed on me. Wanted to sit up; that's all it would take and my head would be free of the water. The mother goddess stood over me, her hand shimmering with power. The water forced itself into my nose, mouth, and eyes, down into my lungs and belly. Chest expanding with the force, I fought the new panic rising within me.

As the water pressure reached its peak, it whipped away from me and I spun into the air, held aloft by the west wind. It tore at my hair, drew the water from my lungs, and gave me breath. Just as quickly, it stole my breath, collapsing my lungs inward, drawing my life away as I was spun 'round and 'round in a twister that seemed to pull at my very soul. The mother goddess was there one second, and gone the next as I was sent spiraling.

The ground rose and cradled me, stopped the spinning. I clung to the earth, buried my hands into its strength and comfort. This was home; this was where I belonged.

"Reach for your power now, child. Once you leave my embrace, anger will be the key. As you grow and learn, you will adapt to connect when other emotions fill you. But for now, your fury will be your strength."

I didn't hesitate, but did as she said. The power was there, a lightly humming tune I couldn't quite make out . . . yet it called to me. I reached for it with everything in me, from my hand stretching outward, to my soul reaching for it, brushing against the spirit and power of the earth. Twinning around one another, the connection rippled all the way through me. My body was cushioned by the wet sand and I stared up at the sky, no longer in pain. No longer questioning what the mother goddess would show me. Slowly, I stood and faced the mother goddess. "There is something else, isn't there?"

She lifted her hand, trailing it down the edge of my face, letting it hover over my heart. "You carry Spirit as well as Earth, and that is dangerous. Spirit, the one element that can control all the others . . . it is a double-edged sword. If you use it, as Cassava has, your soul will begin to shatter. Pieces of it used up until you are no longer yourself, but a shallow, dark imitation. And those you use it on? What do you think happens to them?"

I frowned, considering my own situation, my father's, and even Ash, who I knew was manipulated by Cassava. "Paranoia."

"Yes, the heart that fears cannot trust, even those who it loves. Where there is fear, love cannot reside." The mother goddess looked past me, out into the water. "Spirit was never meant to be used as a weapon, and so it breaks those who wield it thusly."

She turned to me, and the conversation shifted again. Her smile warmed her face, and her long hair swirled around her, teasing the top of her shoulders. "Child, you are my chosen one. You will bring your family back to their glory. They believe their power is of growing things, of manipulating plants and conversing with animals. They have forgotten their ties are to everything this earth offers."

"I don't understand."

She held a hand over the sand and it swirled up in a lazy loop, bits of sparkling quartz and silicone catching the light. "Every particle of the earth is yours to command. When you understand that, you will be in your full power. The earth is the womb of all that IS. It births everything. You will see, fear not. The trials you face will shape and teach you. They must. Or your family and our world will die."

Chills swept over me. "No pressure there." My home called to me, tugging on my body and heart. "I think I need to go back now." Yet I wasn't totally sure. What would happen if I stayed? Could I stay with her?

"Yes, you do. There is much to be done to cleanse the world of those who do it harm." With a single nod, I turned and walked away. My testing was complete. I was an Ender.

I thought when my testing was finished, and having gained the approval of the mother goddess, I would be able to connect to my abilities whenever I wanted. That I would finally be like the other elementals and no longer the useless outsider I was raised to believe.

Apparently, not so much. I stood thigh-deep in the water of the testing room, the damp heat from the underground hot spring curling around my naked body, caressing my skin, and making me shiver. Above my head, the stalactites hung low, moisture dripping from them into the pool. I couldn't quite bring myself to step out of the water, though. I wasn't ready to go fully back to the world that awaited me.

I stood there, fingers trailing in the water as my mind wandered.

Already the experience on the other side of the hot springs within the mother goddess's embrace was fading, and I struggled with my insecurities. My whole life I'd been the weak one, the one everyone mocked for my inability. I'd been the one sent to the Planting fields, and even in that I'd failed. And now the mother goddess told me I was her chosen one . . . "Can't exactly tell her that I decline, either," I murmured. No, one did not tell the mother goddess, 'no thanks, I think I'll pass. Choose someone else to help you.'

Swallowing hard, I held my hand over the water. My feet were half-buried in the hot spring sand. The display the mother goddess had put on, swirling the sand through the air, had fascinated me. Maybe I could do the same. I reached for the power of the earth, cringing just before I connected, unable to make myself grab hold of it. The pain was still too real to me.

"Damn." I put a hand to my head, rubbing at my temple. The mother goddess's voice whispered across the water to me.

"Child, it will be many moons before you can fully break the bonds Cassava has placed on your soul. Be patient with yourself. Be kind to yourself."

I rolled my eyes so I could stare at the darkness and stalactites above. The conditioning I'd endured had come close to severing my connection to the earth completely. I didn't know how close, but I suspected there were more than just my family's lives in the countdown to destroy the lung burrowers. Had that only been a few weeks ago? Cassava had come close to tearing our entire family apart, nearly killed my father, and had weakened our home by wiping out nearly all of the Enders.

All so she could reign as she saw fit, without anyone to naysay her. The only good thing that had come out of the situation was the training I'd been put through. Becoming an Ender had started me on a path to finding out the truth about myself, my abilities, and the secrets of the past.

I shivered again as my body recalled, all too clearly, the pain when mother goddess severed Cassava's ties to my heart, body, and soul.

In my time with her, I felt like I'd been stripped to the marrow of my soul.

Flicking my hands across the top of the water, I sent my mind along another path, one that didn't give me the heebie-jeebies.

The last few months still seemed unreal in quiet moments of reflection. I'd gone from being a lowly Planter in the fields, to training to become an Ender—one of the king's elite guards—faced down my stepmother Cassava, saved my family from the lung burrowers, and now I'd finished my testing. Something I thought I would never do with my lack of power. I looked around, finally taking note of the beach in front of me. The torches that had lit my path to the hot spring had gone out—except for one.

How long had I been in the water?

Flickering and dancing on a breeze that swept down through the halls above, the last flame beckoned me. A hand-like flare reached out, curling fiery fingers toward the beach. I stepped back. Growing and shifting, the flame leapt from the torch, forming itself into a fire tiger.

The big cat stalked toward me, its coat rippling in the unseen breeze, stripes going from a deep blue glow to a strange green and back again. As beautiful as it was, though, I wasn't getting any closer.

I took a few steps back into the water. "I don't suppose you just want to talk, do you, kitty?"

The tiger opened its mouth and roared, a fire storm shooting toward me. I fell back into the hot spring, the water rushing over my head. I stared upward as I sunk into the embrace of the water, while the flames rushed over the surface. Distorted and muted, they still illuminated the hot springs the way human fireworks lit the skies several times a year.

I kicked back, pushing myself deeper before lifting my head out of the water. Twenty feet from the shoreline now, the water steaming hot around me, I tread the surface.

I couldn't resist. "Here, kitty, kitty."

The tiger roared again, flames licking across the distance, dying before they touched me. The big cats were always tied to a fire elemental, or a Salamander as we called them. And seeing how I had killed a few of them in the fight to save my family only weeks ago, I was betting they still weren't happy with me.

But that was just a guess.

The big cat swatted at the sand, sending sparkling hot tiny embers into the water. Maybe not so much a guess, after all.

Putting the fire tiger's flame out to get to the shore was possible, but I would have to call on the earth and use the power newly opened to me.

"Couldn't I have at least gotten a day or two to get used to using my abilities?" I licked my lips, tasting the minerals and salt from the water. I lifted one hand and focused on the ground under the tiger's pacing feet. Wet and heavy, the sand would douse the fire perfectly.

If I could make it happen and push past my own hang-ups.

The power of the earth hummed just out of reach. "Come on," I whispered. "Just grab it."

Fear, icy cold and jarring despite the heat of the hot spring, shot through my body and stabbed at my thoughts. The pain was almost as bad as before, mind numbing in its strength. Cassava had done her work well. I lowered my hand and scissor kicked my legs, swimming backward. "You win this time, cat."

I reached the far side of the hot spring and pulled myself up on the slick, warm rocks. Shame burned in my gut. On the far shoreline the tiger paced and snarled, its body swirling as the fire flicked off its coat.

Someone had sent the cat to hurt me, to get back at me for what had happened in the Pit, of that much I was sure. I closed my eyes, the memories swirling up and around. I could almost smell smoke and sulfur that had been underneath everything we touched, could feel my spear shiver as I slammed it into the Enders we'd faced. Killing another Ender was a death sentence, one I'd barely escaped. But it looked like I wasn't out of the fire just yet.

I opened my eyes to see the tiger gone and moved back into the water.

Voices floated down the stairs. "She's still in her testing, we don't know how long it will take. You know that!" My tester who'd sent me into the hot springs to meet the mother goddess, Douglas if I remembered his name right, did not sound happy. At least he was trying to defend me to whomever he was with.

"I don't care if she's still naked and shaking from the touch of the mother goddess, she is going to trial for her crimes. She thinks she is above the law. As an Ender, she is more subject to it than any other. Her training makes her deadly. She is a weapon not to be used for anything other than protection. Her head will roll before this is over." That voice was familiar, but hard to place with the way it bounced across the water. Female, and husky, I tried to place it but failed. There was no woman I knew in our family with that raspy of a voice.

Sliding along the rocks, I pushed under an overhanging shelf so I could watch without being seen. The mist rising off the hot spring continued to flow upward, helping to hide me. But it meant I couldn't see as well as I'd hoped, either.

Two figures came to a stop on the beach. They argued in low tones and finally it seemed that Douglas had enough. His back was to me and he was blocking my view of his companion. Douglas put a hand on the other figure's chest and shoved. Silently, I cheered.

"Tester, you are going to get yourself killed."

"Then you are no better than what you are accusing our princess of."

I sucked in a sharp breath. No one in our family had ever called me a princess, even though it was true. A spot warmed in my heart and I clutched my arms around myself as if to hold it there. If nothing else, I would hold this moment to me.

Douglas had his hands in the air, and his back to me physically blocking the other person. "Get out of here. She isn't out yet. You can see that."

"She has completed the testing. I know she has set foot on the sand." A booby trap. The cat was set to attack me and alert its master as soon as my feet touched the ground.

"You don't know that," Douglas shouted, his voice bouncing off the walls in the cavern.

Finally, I got a good look at his companion. Bright red hair visible, even across the water and through the mist. And I knew without seeing her orange eyes.

Magma had come looking for me.

Green shit sticks, this really was not a good turn of events. I leaned out so I could get a better look. Magma strode across the sand, her black leather Ender body suit clinging to her. She stopped with her feet at the edge of the water. "I will wait for her here. I don't want her slipping past us again."

Douglas looked like he was going to have a fit. "Get out, Ender Magma. I will bring her to you when her testing is done."

"No."

They continued to argue and I knew there was no way to get past them. At least, not across the shoreline. A shiver ran through my body as a cool breeze from deeper in the caverns blew across the water. Freezing wasn't going to help me any. Slowly, I slid back into the hot spring, careful not to make a sound, the heat flushing my skin and body.

My hair spun out around me, floating on the surface like golden seaweed. Using the rocky edge of the pool, I pulled myself back into the shadows of the overhanging rock. How the hell was I going to get out of this?

"What is going on here?" My father's voice boomed across the water to me. I spun around, the water swirling into eddies about my body.

"Ender Magma thinks to pull Larkspur from her testing to be tried at the Pit." Douglas's voice held more than a hint of condescension.

"She needs to be properly tried, Basileus. You convincing the ambassador she did nothing wrong is not enough for Queen Fiametta. She wants Larkspur properly tried, and punished. As is the queen's right."

Someone, I assumed Douglas, sucked in a breath so hard I heard it all the way across the water. I knew why.

Magma had called my father by name, and not used "your highness" or even "king." It was a slap in the face. Below us, the earth growled, and even from where I hid, I saw the subtle glow of green on my father's hands. The rocks under me rumbled, and the water rippled with the vibrations. Magma treaded very dangerous ground.

I let go of the rocks so I could float free in the water.

"Magma. You forget yourself. I will bring Larkspur to Fiametta myself." His words were laced with granite and power. I shivered and was pleased to see that not only did Magma leave, but Douglas, too. I waited until their figures disappeared up the stairs cut into the earth before I swam across the water, keeping my movements as stealthy as possible. But he still heard me.

"Larkspur. Get dressed."

"Are you going to hand me over to them?" I reached the shore and stood, the water lapping around my thighs. My feet sunk into the sand, putting me eye level with my father.

Everything about him reminded me that he was the king. The flecks of gray through his dark brown hair were a mark of age most of our people didn't see, the deep green of his eyes were filled with knowledge of the past, present, and future, and the power I could see dancing along his fingertips like green flames made the earth hum under my feet.

He flicked his fingers at me, a move that would have the sand push me forward. This was a gift I had—the ability to see when another elemental would use their power. It had saved me more than once already.

I sidestepped the push and stepped fully onto the shoreline. "I'll take that as a yes."

He shook his head. "Lark, I would not hand over any of my children to Fiametta. She is a friend of Cassava. They are very close, in fact." His eyes softened and he got a faraway look that scared me more than if he'd been angry and yelling.

I swallowed hard as I watched the emotions play across his face. "You still love her?"

His eyes narrowed. "She is the mother of most of my children. I cannot hate her."

"Yet, she tried to kill you, me, and did kill a number of our family. She killed my mother and Bram. So while you might not hate her, I do." I strode past him to where my clothes were piled. There were flecks of sand over them and I shook out the leather vest and snug fitting cotton pants quickly before putting them back on.

"She . . . is still in my head, Lark." He spoke softly and I spun, startled.

"What do you mean?"

"Years, years of damage and manipulation. I cannot always tell what is a real memory and what is fabricated." He wiped a hand over his face. "Be patient with me. I am trying to change things." The mother goddess had said much the same. But it was hard. He was my father, the king, and I wanted him to be strong enough to just be . . . okay.

The mother goddess's words reverberated through me. The power of Spirit, like the ring Cassava had worn and used, destroyed not only those the power touched, but those who controlled it as well. Losing their ability to trust.

Though I had the ability to use Spirit, the more I learned about it, the more I didn't want anything to do with it.

I didn't want to become Cassava.

"I will try to be patient, but then you have to trust me to see things you don't," I said.

My father grunted. "Something in particular?"

"You know Cassava won't stop until she has your throne and those who stand in her way are dead. You said she is friendly with Fiametta. How do you know this isn't Cassava pushing her friend to call me in to trial only to kill me?"

"Fiametta wants your head, regardless. You broke into her home, Lark. You showed up all her Enders, and stole away using one of their Traveling armbands. You made her look like a fool and the other leaders know it."

With my fingers on the buckles of my vest, I tightened each one slowly. "So she wants to make herself look better?"

He nodded. "In essence, yes."

"And Cassava? You do remember she tried to kill you, only a few weeks ago." I wasn't sure I could handle the thought of him not remembering. My whole life had been a mishmash of broken and stolen memories. I didn't want that for my father, and now that Cassava was gone, he could maybe finally have his mind back.

At the sound of footsteps, I knew our conversation would shift. Around others, my father treated me like the bastard child I was; like I was less than everyone else. Alone together, as rare as it was, was the only time I saw the father I remembered from my childhood. The one who loved me despite my bastard status.

He arched an eyebrow and stood a little straighter. "You make it sound like you are important enough to be bothered with. You forget that while you may have saved our family from the old queen, that was a fluke. Don't ever forget your place, Larkspur. You are an Ender now. You are replaceable." He turned and strode up the shoreline, a flick of his hand indicating that I should follow him.

Replaceable.

The funny thing was I wasn't more than a few steps up from useless. A smile flickered over my lips until I saw who was waiting for father at the far side of the hot springs. Long dark brown hair so like her mother's cascaded over her shoulders all the way to the backs of her knees. Her gray eyes glanced over at me and she arched an eyebrow. No words were needed. We didn't like each other. She was too much like her mother.

And I was too much like mine.

She slipped her hand into Father's and he gave her a gentle smile. The oldest of my siblings was also the best at making it look like she was an obedient child despite the truth of her wild ways.

I whispered her name as if in doing so I could make her disappear. "Belladonna."

Chapter 2

I managed to get to the kitchens in the Spiral without being seen. I don't know how long I'd been in the mother goddess's embrace, but I'd been without food and water and my reserves were stretched thin enough that I didn't think I'd make it to the Enders barracks to eat. I must have been gone at least a day by the way my stomach growled at me to hurry up.

Platters of leftovers from the king's table the night before were stacked up. I grabbed a plate and shoveled food onto it in large quantities. Potatoes, leeks, radishes, trout, and a fresh green salad with dandelions were the first helping. I sat in a corner, eating quickly, barely tasting the food; just filling my stomach as fast as I could.

"A drink to go with it, perhaps?" A goblet was thrust under my nose, the heady scent of honey mead making my mouth water.

I took the goblet, and lifted my eyes to see a familiar face.

"Niah, what are you doing here?" The storyteller hadn't made an appearance since she'd stirred things up months ago. Things that had ultimately sent me to the Ender's barracks. Looking back, I realized she'd done what she'd done on purpose. Like a lot of storytellers, she was part seer as well. Or at least, she claimed to be.

"I like food. Most storytellers do, you know. They eat, and as they eat, they think up new ways to spin their words." She plucked a bunch of grapes off a plate and popped one into her mouth. She poured a second cup of the honey mead for herself and took a sip. I licked my lips, the sweet flavor lingering nicely. The mead tasted thick and lovely on my tongue.

"So what tale have you got for me this time? Last time you nearly had me with my head on the chopping platter."

She smiled and the hint of violet in her eyes glimmered, the mark of a shape shifter. Not a common ability amongst our family. "Oh, nothing much. Rumors abound you know."

That stopped me in mid-shovel. "What kind of rumors?"

"Oh, that Cassava is working through the other families, trying to make trouble."

I stuffed my fork into my mouth and talked around the food. "Nothing new there."

"No?" Niah tipped her head back and gulped the mead as if it were water. "I wouldn't be so sure. May I make a suggestion?"

I waved a hand at her, but kept eating with the other. "Be my guest."

"Your stepmother is a tricky devil. I believe she will go to ground for some time to let the 'heat' as the humans say, die. That doesn't mean her tools won't be used, though, and her plans abandoned."

While the advice was good, it wasn't something I hadn't already considered. "How about an actual story, Niah. Something I can think about while I'm on trial at the Pit."

Her eyes widened. "Your father surely won't let you be taken."

I shrugged then leaned back in my chair. "Don't be so sure he has a choice. What would he do if the other leaders spoke against him? They could cite the rules. We all know what I did as an Ender . . . never mind. A story. Please?"

Niah tapped her fingers against her lips. "For you child, a story of the Deep and the ocean the Undines rule."

I hadn't heard an Undine story since I truly was a child. "Of the Kraken that protects them?"

She laughed. "Are you telling this story or am I?"

I waved her to go ahead while I dished up another plate of food.

Niah's voice lowered until she was barely whispering, and the atmosphere in the room seemed to darken with it. "The Undines have a legend that the child of the Kraken will one day rule, and under his guidance they will see their family raised above all others."

I smiled; every family had a story about a chosen one. Even ours. My smile faltered as the mother goddess's words bounced around in my head. *"You are my chosen one."*

My food suddenly didn't seem so palatable, and I pushed my plate away.

Niah didn't seem to notice.

"The Kraken will rise in the face of great evil, and help its child rule. But not before so much blood spills that the waters of the Deep darken, and the fish disappear, and the air stills. These are all signs that the Kraken's child is upon them. Each of the Undine's three bloodlines believe they will produce the Kraken's child. But I will tell you now, it is not the warriors with their green-tinged hair, nor the shape shifters with their violet eyes, nor even the healers. No, it will be a true child of the water, a child born of all three lines. Blue hair and pale skin, with eyes of the clearest ocean waves; that is the child you must seek if you want to meet the Kraken's chosen heir. And so the legend is told."

"And what happens when this child is never born?" I couldn't help poking at her, just a little.

She gave a snort and waved her hand, the mood dispelled. "Don't be foolish. The child of the Kraken will come. Though hopefully not in my lifetime."

"Why not?"

"Change is not easy for those of us who have lived this long. You, you will have no problem with change." Again, she waved at me. "Now, a token to go along with your story."

She wiggled her fingers at me and something shiny and hooked flew over them, dancing back and forth several times before it came to rest in the palm of her hand. "Here." Niah held it out to me. "I think you will need this very soon."

I peered into her hand and gingerly held up a fishing hook, barbed on one end, and a tiny blue diamond sitting at the top where the line would be set. "What will I need this for?"

She smiled, took the hook and lifted it to my ear. "Hold still." I flinched as she jammed it through the cartilage. "There, very pretty."

Gingerly, I ran a finger over the new earring I sported. "Thank you?"

Niah popped another grape in her mouth and sauntered away. "Just you wait and see, Ender, you will thank me. Just you wait and see."

After finishing my meal, I went straight to my father's private rooms. The moss thick under my feet, cushioning my steps as I moved in farther—albeit a bit reluctantly.

"Lark, there is only one way to keep you safe. You may not like it, but you will do as I say in this." His green eyes flicked to mine as if to judge my reaction. I nodded, though my mind raced with possibilities.

"Of course."

He waited as if I were going to retract my words. "Good. You will be going into the Deep with your sister. I believe a civil war is brewing, and my contacts have disappeared. You will do two things while you are there. The first, find our ambassador. Dead or alive, Barkley has information I need. Do you understand?"

I nodded, a steady thrum of excitement and nerves building in my gut. My first assignment . . . even if the reason for it was because I was in over my head in worm guts, it didn't really matter. This was to be my life, as an Ender, helping the king and making sure his ambassadors were safe.

"If Barkley is dead, then find his room and search it. Just be wary, his lover is an Undine. Do you understand?"

I hate to admit my jaw dropped. "His lover is an Undine? And you knew?" Half-breeds like me were not common, and the higher up your station, the more likely you were to be forced to marry as you were told. Which, of course, was why it was all that much worse that my father broke his own rules by bedding my mother who was anything but an earth elemental.

My father frowned at me. "I approved, yes. You'll understand when you meet them."

I nodded again, though I wasn't sure how I could understand him approving a relationship that would produce a half-breed. I wouldn't wish that life on any child. "And the other thing?"

"You will protect the ambassador I'm sending with you at all costs. I have not decided who is to be my heir to the throne, but she is in the running. As are all of my children."

The door slammed open and Belladonna strode in. "Surely you don't mean all your children, do you, Father? No one would stand behind a bastard on the throne."

Belladonna's voice might have been smooth as silk worms spinning their threads, but it grated over my ears. I straightened, my vertebrae cracking and popping. Not that I'd been slouching, but I refused to look like I was taking any crap from her.

And then her words and my father's hit me. If Belladonna was here, she was the one Father was talking about. For a stupid moment, I'd believed I was taking Briar with me. Why couldn't it have been sweet, kind Briar?

"Belladonna," Father said her name softly, "try to be kind. She is still your sister."

Belladonna sniffed the air as if something stunk, her gray eyes narrowing. "I am always kind. Ask your people, Father, they'll tell you I am nothing but sweetness and light."

I lifted an eyebrow. "More like you terrorize the children when you think no one is looking. Giving them nightmares with stories of lung burrowers coming to eat their hearts if they don't bow to you when you go by."

She stomped her foot, fists clenched at her side, her demeanor slipping. "You sneaky ugly weevil! What are you doing, following me around? I will take you outside and beat you as you should have been beaten years ago!"

I stepped toward her, using my height to an advantage, looking down at her. "Belladonna, say the word. Say it."

Father cleared his throat and put his hands between us, gently shoving us apart.

"Girls, whether you like it or not—and I see by your faces you do not—you are going to work together." We stood across from him but as far apart from each other as possible. Belladonna was as opposite to me in looks as she was in personality. She was petite and curvy and had long dark brown hair and light gray eyes. The top of her head barely came to my chin, but her looks weren't really what concerned me.

No, she was her mother's daughter, through and through. I knew she was lying when she said Cassava had tricked her too. But our father wouldn't hear me say a word against her, or any of my siblings, for that matter.

Belladonna smiled sweetly. "But Larkspur is so new to being an Ender. Wouldn't it be better if someone more experienced came with me? Someone . . . like Ash?"

My whole body stiffened. I'd seen his memories of her and if I was anything of a friend to him, I couldn't let him get sucked into this. "Ash can't go. He's running things here for Father." My voice was sharp and I struggled not to yell at her. I had seen too clearly how she had treated Ash in the past.

As if saying his name had called him, my senior Ender and mentor stepped into the room. Dressed in the dark brown leather vest and lighter brown cotton pants of our order, he cut quite the figure. Even I could admit that about him. Dark blond hair and honey-colored eyes gave Ash an exotic look in a family of elementals where dark hair and eyes were prevalent. He gave my father a quick nod. "Your Majesty, the ambassador and her Ender from the Pit are waiting for you in the throne room." He didn't look at me, or Belladonna, but stared straight ahead.

My father let out a sigh. "Daughters. You will do as I ask. Belladonna, you are the acting ambassador. I want to know all you can decipher about the two who are battling for the Deep's throne. From what I understand, they are both children of King Marianas, do your homework on them before you go. You will promise them nothing, understand?" His eyes flicked to mine. "And you will protect your sister."

As if my life was worthless. But I knew that wasn't the case, as much as the words stabbed at me. He had to have a way to get me out of the Rim long enough to defuse the situation with the Pit. Our fiery cousins might be good at reining in their tempers, but when they finally blew their tops . . . the world was not a safe place for anyone. Especially not the person they were pissed at, which in this case was me.

Father strode from the room, the carpet of grass muffling any sound his steps made. Ash snapped his fingers then pointed at Belladonna and me. "You two, meet me at the Traveling room in one hour."

"Gladly, pet," Belladonna purred, and I had to fight the sudden urge to reach over and strangle her.

With a swish of her skirts, she sashayed past Ash. At the last second she ran a hand down his arm. "I wish you were the one coming with me. At least then I'd know I was safe."

She couldn't see his face, but I could. He swallowed hard, as if he were trying not to vomit. "Princess, thank you for the compliment, but I've trained Larkspur. She will do her job," he said, but the revulsion was in his eyes. Rape is not something our people condoned in the least, but as Ash had said, who would believe the princess had forced him to pleasure her?

No one but me. I knew my family too well not to believe him.

"Ash, hold on," I said, "I want to speak to my father." I didn't stay for Ash's answer, just ran after the receding figure of my father.

I caught up to him just before he reached the throne room. "Father. Wait, please." He stopped and glanced back at me.

"Larkspur, I do not have time for this."

He was right, there was no time, but that didn't mean I wasn't going to try and fix what I already knew was going to be an epic disaster. There was no way Belladonna and I could work together.

"Send Raven instead. Belladonna will make things worse in the Deep. I know that."

"Belladonna is trained to be an ambassador, you are not. How would you know who would be best to send?" His voice rose in intensity with each word, his eyes flashing with emotion.

I refused to back down. "She is her mother's daughter. You don't know she isn't still doing as Cassava wishes. And it's not my fault that I wasn't trained as she was! I could have been if I were treated as your daughter and not as some outcast cur!" I snapped at him. His eyes widened, then narrowed with a speed that made me doubt the hurt I'd seen in them.

"You go too far, Ender. Remember your place. A princess by blood? Perhaps. But not by any other standard." He stepped through the door and into the throne room, slamming it behind him.

Stunned, the shock of his words slowly filtered through me as I stared at the closed door. Once more, put in my place by someone who was supposed to love me unconditionally. I made my way back to my father's rooms where Ash waited for me. He took a single look at me, but asked no questions as to what I'd needed to speak to the king about. I wondered what he saw when he looked at me. What did my face give away? I hoped nothing, but I had a feeling Ash saw far more than I wanted.

I didn't know what to say, how to break the growing silence between us.

Ash looked me over again. "Testing went well?"

I nodded, grateful he broke the awkward quiet. Grateful he hadn't heard my father speak to me like I was still nothing to him. Was this part of the act to keep me safe, or did he really mean what he'd said? I might not ever know. I replayed Ash's question in my head. "Yes, I guess the testing went well. I wouldn't know if it hadn't, would I?"

"You wouldn't be here so quickly if it had gone south." He turned and beckoned for me to follow. "A week is a fairly short time to be in the mother goddess's embrace."

I stumbled to a stop. "A week? I was gone a whole week?" At least that explained the gnawing hunger and thirst. The whole time with the mother goddess had felt like hours. And though the pain part had seemed to last longer, I was already forgetting it.

He glanced over his shoulder at me. "My testing, I was gone ten days. If you had taken longer than a month we would assume you were lost. Our bodies can't stand to be within her embrace for longer."

Damn, I had no idea that was even possible. "No one told me about that."

"It's not spoken of until you come through. You need to go in blind to the dangers."

I frowned, thinking about the time I'd spent with the mother goddess. None of it had seemed particularly dangerous. Painful, yes, but I never thought I was truly in danger.

Ash led the way through the Spiral, the place my father and his children called home. Our family's version of a castle, it was made up of all species of trees wrapping themselves around one another in a massive spiral that reached through the redwood giants. The interior was far larger than the exterior, driving deep into the earth and expanding beyond reason within the Spiral. A magic older than our family had created it and its expansive nature. The hot springs were in the lowest level of the Spiral, protected and used only for healing and testing.

We weren't going to another room within the Spiral, though. The Traveling room where we would meet Belladonna was in the Enders barracks.

We exited the Spiral, the redwoods swaying above us, the soft sound of the trees moving in time with the wind. Several birds called down to us as we stepped into the sunlight, but Ash never slowed as we strode to the Ender's barracks. I wanted him to slow down. I wanted to just . . . be by him. We had been through a lot together and I felt like I finally had a friend I could be myself around. Someone who didn't care I was a bastard, or that I would never be a real princess. "Belladonna specifically asked that you be assigned to her."

Ash stopped mid-stride, and only because I knew what to look for did I see the way his shoulders tightened. "And your father, what did he say?" He didn't look at me, so I could only guess at the expression on his face. I went with horror.

"I told her you were too busy running things. That you couldn't go. My father probably would have let her take you if I hadn't said something." I walked past him. The main training room was empty except for Blossom practicing with her dual short swords in the corner, so I wasn't worried about who might hear me.

"What, do you want me to thank you?" Ash bit out and it was my turn to tense.

I turned to face him, and crossed my arms. "Ash, we're friends. Friends thank one another for sticking their necks out. So yeah, it wouldn't kill you. Unless you wanted to go with her?"

He snorted and shook his head. "Get your things, Larkspur. You have a princess to protect and I still have to brief you."

Without another word, he walked away, taking the stairs into the belly of the barracks where the Traveling room was hidden. He said nothing about being my friend. Perhaps I was wrong about that too. Wouldn't surprise me, it seemed lately my ability to figure out men had slid into the compost heap. A sigh of frustration escaped me before I could catch it.

"Lark, where are you going? You just got back." Blossom slid her two swords into the sheaths at her side with a soft shush of metal on leather. We were the only two female Enders left after the lung burrowers had swept through wiping out nearly half of our family.

"I'm on assignment, I guess. I have to watch over Belladonna."

Blossom made a face, her lips and nose crinkling in tandem. I more than agreed with her, but kept my own facial muscles still. "Be careful, I don't want to be the only girl here to keep the men in line." She gave me a wink and went back to her practicing. Not so long ago, she was thinking of quitting, but I'd convinced her to stay. I was glad I had. Maybe in Blossom I'd finally find a true friend. But not today.

"You be careful too." I jogged away, down the main hall to the living quarters and into my tiny room. Barely big enough for the bed and table beside it, I was surprised that someone was waiting for me.

Coal.

His raven-black hair glistened as he lifted his head, the blue-black highlights catching the light. His green eyes roved over me, a hunger in their depths. I swallowed hard. Knowing him as well as I did, I was very aware of what he wanted and despite my growing understanding that I had to cut him loose, my body responded to him. It knew the tune we played "oh-so-well" together.

"Lark," his voice was husky and full of desire.

Steeling myself, I kept my voice even. "Coal, I have an assignment. I have to go."

With his one remaining hand, he reached for me. "Can't they find someone else? I've been lonely without you. I don't want you to go."

"I've only been gone a week." I dodged his hand and went to my knees so I could get at the weapons under my bed. In particular, my spear that had belonged to my mother—there was no way I was leaving it behind when I was going into danger.

His hand dropped to my head, digging into my thick hair and tugging at me lightly, bringing my face close to his knees. "Lark, I've missed you. Doesn't that count for something?"

I sat back, spear in one hand and three knives in the other. A part of me expected to feel something other than desire—a pull of my heart toward him. But there was nothing other than the zings of lust, and even with the guilt that ate at me, that wasn't enough. I had to let him go. Had to make him move on. "I'm sorry, Coal, I have to leave. I have an assignment."

His eyes hardened, flashing with anger. "Right. And that has nothing to do with this." He held up my necklace with the griffin tooth dangling from it. The necklace was a gift from Griffin, the wolf shifter who lived on the southern outskirts of our forest. He'd given me the necklace to stave off the lung burrowers while I fought off Cassava.

I reached for it. "I have to return that."

"Not according to this." Coal fumbled with the necklace and pulled a piece of paper from under his shirt, reading from it. "Larkspur, keep the necklace for your next trip, it looks better on you than it ever did on me. But I want it back when you return. Your friend, Griffin."

I lifted my eyebrows. "So?"

"A man doesn't just give a gift to a woman without expecting something in return. Or maybe he's making a payment for something he's already had."

My jaw dropped. He just called me a whore. I curled my fingers into a fist and pulled my arm back. A hand behind me grabbed me before I could ram my fist into Coal's face.

"Lark, I said I needed you in the Traveling room," Ash said.

I let out a slow breath, reached out and jerked the necklace from Coal's fingers. Guilt over cutting off his hand be damned. I didn't need this worm shit trying to control me. He wasn't getting the subtle cues; time to be blunt. "Get out of here, and don't bother missing me. We're done."

His green eyes seemed to burn, and the ugliness that hid behind his good looks reared its head. "You're a slut, just like Belladonna. Just like your mother."

Ash grunted as if he'd been hit in the gut. I swallowed hard and knew what I was about to say would sever the ties between Coal and me once and for all. There would be no going back. But I just didn't want to deal with his garbage anymore, or the guilt. "I should have cut off your head instead of your hand, you stupid ass." To be fair, I'd cut it off because I'd had no other choice. He'd been under Cassava's compulsion and was dragging me to her so she could kill me.

But to Coal, the reason wouldn't matter.

I pushed past Ash and strode toward the Traveling room, leaving a stunned Coal and silent Ash behind.

I should have known better than to think Coal would let me go after dropping that little bombshell. I made it all the way to the stairwell leading down to the Traveling room. A shout from Ash was the only warning I got. Coal came at me hard, leaping from the first step. He tackled me, and we fell in a tangled heap, hitting the sharp edges of the stairs cut into the earth. He screamed at me, his voice a blur of words and anger, violence and profanities flowing out of him.

There was nothing I could say, nothing I wanted to say. At the bottom of the stairs he got on top of me, pinning me with his knees as he tried to choke me with his one hand. A futile effort. I batted his hand away and sat up, pushing him off. "Go home, Coal. You aren't needed here."

Useless.

The word hung in the air as if I'd said it. He wasn't useless, but he sure as hell couldn't do the job he loved anymore, he couldn't guard the edge of the Rim. And that was my fault.

"You bitch, you cut my hand off." He breathed hard, as if he had been running for hours.

"Cassava was using you—"

"Shut up! You . . . I can't believe you. No, you're covering for someone." He was nodding, wagging one finger at me. I shook my head, but he was on a roll. "Yes, that's what's going on. You're covering for someone. This Griffin, was he the one? Or maybe"—he spun and looked at Ash who'd caught up to us—"You! You cut my hand off."

"Oh, for the sake of the mother goddess, Coal!" I grabbed his arm and slapped his face hard. "Go home."

He stumbled away, looking between Ash and me. "You are trying to steal her from me. But Lark will always come back to me. I'm her first love. Her heart is mine." He spat at us, then finally turned and stumbled up the stairs. The silence that fell between Ash and me was not comfortable and I squirmed. Damn, I wished I could back up this day a few hours and start it again.

"I don't know what's gotten into him. It's like he's losing himself."

Ash nodded. "It happens sometimes when a limb is cut off like that, almost like a piece of their minds goes with it."

I bent and picked up the necklace, slipping it over my head. "You've seen this before, when someone loses a limb?"

"Yes, two Enders. They just couldn't function as they had before and they made up a reality they could live with."

"What happened to them?" I was more than a little afraid of the answer.

"Banished. Neither could be helped, and they began to threaten the safety of the family. Enough of that, you need to understand what you're getting into when you step into the Deep."

Relief swept through me. I might be going into a difficult situation, but I was leaving behind a mess with Coal. A mess I knew was far from cleaned up. Time would help, time apart; I had to believe Coal would find someone else, but I knew the struggle of being pegged "useless." Our family wasn't so good at taking care of lame ducks.

We went into the Traveling room, and again I was struck by the sheer wonder and magic of it. Set up as a globe, the whole world was contained in the one room. But instead of looking down on a globe, we looked from the inside out, and the walls of the room were seemingly painted with the continents and oceans. The currents of water and air were visible as they flowed around us, my feet splashing in the Pacific Ocean's reflection. This was how we moved around the world without dealing too much with the humans.

Ash finally looked at me. His eyes burrowed into mine and I struggled to breathe. Unspoken words hovered in the air between us, and I couldn't stand the silence. "What?"

"I'm glad you made it out of your testing. I need you, Lark."

A lightning bolt of heat shot through me with his words, and I made myself breathe normally. Fought to think about the reality of what he meant. He didn't mean he needed me other than to help him, I knew that. We were friends. "Running things here getting to you already?"

His eyes didn't leave mine. "Something like that. The trainees are struggling. None of them really want to be Enders. But they're all we have. You and I are the only Enders in truth, so try not to get yourself killed."

I laughed, expecting him to join me.

He didn't.

He pointed to the globe at the water off the southeastern section of the North American continent. "This is where the Deep is situated. The humans call it the Bermuda triangle, and right now we can't Travel directly to it."

"Why not?"

"The civil war going on there is reaching a fever pitch and they've blocked anyone from Traveling directly in or out. Which means you need to go here"—he pointed at an island close to the Deep. Bermuda. Hmm.

"And once we're there?"

"You'll have to row out to the Deep and ask permission to enter."

"Why do I get the feeling you aren't telling me something important?" I put my hand out and touched the spot where the Deep was. The image grew until it took up nearly half the room. A swirl of mist hovered over it, blocking it from view. I pushed the image back, letting the globe return to its normal room-filling size.

"They may decide not to let you in. And if they do that, you could be in trouble."

"Like try to kill us trouble?" I stared at him, watching for signs he held back. He didn't.

"Yes. They might try to kill you, depending on the relationship between them and our ambassador who we believe is already dead, or at the very least, incarcerated in their cells, which are notorious for their own dangers."

My first task was to find the ambassador. "Barkley is his name, isn't it?"

"Yes, and they're saying that whatever happened to him, and we don't know the exact details, was an accident. But the ambassadors from the Pit and the Eyrie have met with 'accidents' too and are missing as well. At the very least, they are all out of contact with their families. Your father thinks they won't dare harm someone of royal blood. But I'm not so sure."

Suddenly dealing with Coal's tantrums and staying close to home sounded like a far better idea than before.

"Too bad I don't have a choice about this," I said softly, reaching out and touching the globe. The water rippled under my hands and Ash nodded.

"You're an Ender now, Lark. Choices are not something you're given. Do as you're told. Keep your charges safe. Protect our family."

Seemingly so simple, yet I knew better. There was nothing simple about being an Ender.

Not a single thing.

Chapter 3

Ash drilled me on the ins and outs of the Deep, or at least as much as he could in the time allotted.

"The humans are afraid of the Deep, Lark, so you will have a hard time getting anyone to take you from the island into deep water. Probably, you will have to row yourself and Belladonna on your own."

I frowned at the spot on the globe that was the Deep. Out in the water, the whole area was covered in a thick fog. I tried pulling the globe closer, but nothing more detailed came up as it should have. Ash stepped behind me. He reached past me, his arm brushing mine, and his body a breath from touching my back. I only had to shift my weight backward and . . . and what? He was my mentor, and I was a new Ender. Not to mention the disaster that was Coal in my life. Why in the seven hells would I complicate things further? Forcing myself to move away from him, I looked to where he pointed.

Spreading my hand out over the section of ocean that was the Deep, I dipped my fingers into the water. "Why are the humans afraid exactly?"

"Humans have a sense of survival and a lot of them have gone missing there. No trace of the boats, no trace of the planes—"

"You mean those flying contraptions?"

"Yes. The Undines don't take well to people encroaching on their territory. They are the worst of us when it comes to strangers. There is something, though, that is not well known. The secret that no one spills unless you have to."

I turned to face him. How much of my own world had been kept from me? Or was this just because I'd been a mere Planter? "What are you talking about?"

"The Undines have slaves. Human slaves."

My eyes felt as though they would pop out of my head. "The mother goddess forbade slavery when she first created us. How are they doing this?" He had to be wrong. I'd been with the mother goddess and she'd even told me slavery was strictly forbidden, that it was an abomination.

"A loophole." Ash stepped back and crossed his arms, which made his biceps flex and pop.

I shook my head as much to clear it as because I couldn't believe what I was hearing. "That can't be right."

"Technically, they get away with it because the humans are considered less than us. The mother goddess forbids us enslaving *one another*. Not the humans." Ash lifted one hand and cupped my chin, stealing my breath. "And they consider half-breeds lower than humans. Be careful they don't realize who you are, Lark. Everyone has heard about the Earth king's weak, half-breed, bastard daughter. If they figure it out, you could end up someone's pet."

His fingers were warm and he slid them along my jaw. I couldn't take my eyes from his. No, this couldn't happen. With a quick jerk, I pulled away. "Then I'll be careful. Thanks for the warning."

He opened his mouth, and then closed it with a slight shake of his head. "If the Undines let you in, I doubt any of us will be able to come after you. You'll be completely on your own. Do you understand?" There was a weight in his eyes that made it hard for me to keep his gaze.

I looked away. "On our own. No matter what happens. I've got it."

"Here, take this with you." He pulled a tiny dagger from his belt. The three-inch blade was honed to an edge so thin it was barely thicker than a blade of grass.

"Why are you giving me this? I have my own daggers and my spear. This looks like it could break with a wrong look sent its way." Ash tucked the tiny blade into its miniscule, equally thin, sheath. With deft fingers he tugged at my vest, unbuckling it quickly. I slapped his hands away. "Hey—"

"Relax, I'm not Coal. You want to keep this blade tucked away. They will frisk you when you get there. Probably take all the weapons you just named. But a small blade like this could go unnoticed. And it won't break. I forged it, so I should know."

I blinked at him stupidly, and stopped fighting him. "You made this knife?"

He slipped his hand inside my vest and worked the knife between the layers of leather where they overlapped. His fingers brushed against the sensitive skin near my belly button and I bit my lip to keep from moving. Toward or away from his hands, I didn't know which I even wanted. Confusion was not something I liked, yet with Ash . . . that seemed to be the state of things.

"Yes. Knowing how to make and repair your own weapons is important. I'll show you when you get back. If you want." He stepped back and gave me a nod, and I let out a sigh of relief.

Pleased that we seemed to be back on friendly terms, I buckled my vest and tried not to think about his hands touching the skin of my belly. "My own private lessons so no one will see me make a mistake?"

Ash grinned, a quick flash of his lips and white teeth before it was gone. "Agreed. But don't tell Belladonna, she'll want lessons for herself just to spite us both."

As if speaking her name had beckoned her, Belladonna swept into the room dressed in full regalia. Her gown trailed behind her, a deep golden hue that offset her skin and dark hair and made her gray eyes stand out. The cut of it was not her usual skintight version of a current fashion human dress, which surprised me. With the empire waist and long flowing skirts that swirled around her feet she looked every inch the princess. Until she opened her mouth.

"Larkspur, I hate this gown. It's ridiculously old fashioned. And the color . . . disgusting." She flicked her fingers against the material while blowing out a rather unladylike snort. "Look at this, it doesn't even lift my breasts, how will I be noticed?"

Good grief, how did I answer that?

Ash stepped out so he could see her. "You aren't there to be noticed, Princess. You're there to act as an ambassador and ferret out information for your king. Nothing more. Did you get your brief on the two supplicants for the Deep's throne?"

The transformation that overcame her was impressive. She took a deep breath forcing her chest up and out, then slid her hands down her body to rest at her waist cinching the material tight, showing off her curves. "Ash, I didn't see you there. Why don't you come with me? I don't think my father will mind. And I would love to have you again." Her words held a double meaning that she couldn't possibly know I understood and they grated down my spine. She took two steps swaying toward him and I just couldn't stand there.

I sidestepped so I completely blocked her. "Leave him alone, Belladonna."

Her eyebrows rose as she tried to move around me. "And why would you care what I do with Ash?"

I went with her, jaw twitching. What I wanted to say was that she'd used him and hurt him enough. But I didn't. "He's in charge here. Show him respect."

She shrugged. "He's not in charge. And neither are you."

Behind her, our father stepped into the Traveling room. "That is correct. *I* am in charge."

Belladonna whirled and swept into a low curtsey, holding it for three breaths before speaking. "Father, I beg you, do not send me with Larkspur. She is inexperienced and I would feel far safer if Ash were at my side."

Damn, it was impressive how fast she could shift directions. One second she was her mother's child, conniving and demanding. The next, humble and begging as if she were truly thinking only of our father's wishes.

Father's eyes flicked from Belladonna to me and then to Ash. They stayed on Ash for more than a few seconds, as if truly weighing Belladonna's request.

Heart in my throat, I waited, hoping he had enough sense to . . . no in a weird way, my sister was right. I was inexperienced and she probably would be safer with Ash. Though he would not be safe with her. Father shook his head.

"No. Larkspur will be your bodyguard. That is final." He beckoned me and I stepped forward. "My daughter's safety will be your first priority, Ender, and you will help her find the information we need to understand if the civil war is dangerous to our family or not. Do not interfere, do not take part in anything other than your duties as an Ender."

I gave him a stiff bow from my waist. "As you say, my king."

He gave me a raised eyebrow and then turned to Belladonna. "You will not put yourself into a situation where your Ender's life could be on the line. When it comes to safety, Larkspur's word will be law between the two of you and you *will* obey her. Do not interfere with the political goings-on and do not take part in anything other than your duties as an ambassador."

Belladonna curtseyed again, and her voice was tight. "As you say, my king."

Father pulled her into a hug. "Be safe, my child."

Letting her go, he left the room as swiftly as he'd entered. My throat tightened as he walked away, closing the door without even a glance behind to me. Ash put a hand on my shoulder, his fingers digging in. Even Belladonna glanced at me and I saw the pity there for just a split second before she covered it. She smoothed her skirts and pointed at the armbands against the wall. The magic that allowed us to travel the world with ease.

"Lark, I believe you are the one who has to use that, correct?"

It took everything I had to swallow the hurt and unshed tears. I was an Ender, I would not cry because my father hadn't hugged me goodbye. But the little girl part of me wanted to sob. Wanted to know why I was so unlovable. Ash's fingers tightened a little more. "Get the armband."

Moving, I felt disconnected from the moment and forced myself to put my hurt away.

The armband was made of cedar, smooth and polished to a high gleam. I slipped it up my arm and settled it over my bicep remembering the last time we'd used the band. "Just to be clear, it won't slide off?"

"No, it won't come off until you remove it, and no one else can take it off unless they remove your arm. I don't suggest you take it off," Ash said. His eyes meeting mine, concern etched around them. "If things go sideways you will have to get out of the radius of the Deep's reach before you can Travel."

Belladonna snorted. "Why would things go sideways? That's ridiculous. We're going as ambassadors. Or at least, I am." She put a hand to her chest and batted her eyes up at Ash.

Choke me with a redwood. I stalked over to her. "Belladonna, we are going into a charged political situation and we all know the other families are not above assassination, blackmail, and regicide. So what makes you think you and I are going to be safe?"

Her gray eyes widened as I spoke and she looked from me to Ash and back again. "Father said it was safe. He wouldn't send me somewhere that wasn't."

Unless he was trying to find a way to get rid of her. A chill swept me from head to toe as the ramifications pinged inside my skull. What better way to remove a snake from the nest than to put it into a watery cave full of hungry sharks? Could that be why he argued with me about Belladonna? Argued that she should go over all the other possible choices?

I didn't want to believe my father was that dastardly, but the possibility was there that he was playing Belladonna. And if he was playing her . . . he could very well be playing me too.

"Let's hope the king is right then." Ash pushed Belladonna and me closer. "Princess, have you Traveled before?"

She nodded, her composure already back in place. "Yes, I have." Of course she had, we'd seen her in the Pit when we'd gone to find the spell that would cure our family from the lung burrowers. Who had taken her then?

The answer hit me hard. Granite. He had been helping Cassava and no doubt had been moving the puzzle pieces around at her request. Including Belladonna and her trip to the Pit. I wanted to ask my sister what she'd been doing there, what messages had she been taking for her mother to Fiametta. Maybe I would get the chance while we were in the Deep. Most likely she would only lie to me, though, so what was the point?

Ash took Belladonna's hands and wrapped them around me, speaking as if she knew nothing. "Hang onto your Ender. Don't let go of her no matter what happens, do you understand?"

Belladonna tightened her arms around my waist, a slight tremor in her hands. "I'm ready."

In that moment, I realized she was afraid. She was scared to go to the Deep, scared that our father might be setting her up to be killed. There was no doubt if it crossed my mind, it had crossed hers. Belladonna was a lot of things, but stupid wasn't one of them.

And I had to admit, I was more than a little afraid myself. What better way to get rid of both of us than to send us into a political hurricane that had already killed multiple ambassadors? Our father would come out smelling like roses, and we would be neatly taken care of without a single smear on the king's character.

My gut clenched. "Ash." Just his name, nothing else. His eyes met mine, honeyed gold and steady as a rock.

"It'll be okay, Lark. And if it's not, I'll come for you both." He stepped back to give us room. The globe around us suddenly seemed bigger and more daunting than when I'd Traveled with him. Touching the island destination, I used my free hand to twist the armband.

Belladonna shivered against me.

And the world around us sucked into a sharp maelstrom of Belladonna's memories.

Worm shit and green sticks, I'd forgotten about this part.

Chapter 4

The blows rained down on her head over and over. "Please, Mother! I didn't mean it." But the pain didn't stop. Belladonna fell to the floor her nose bleeding, tears blurring her vision. Trying to cover up didn't help, hiding only made Mother angrier. She wasn't even sure what she had done wrong. Only that whatever it was had enraged her mother. More often than not, she didn't know what would set off her mother.

Cassava picked her up by a handful of hair. "How dare you even breathe a word to that whore? She is nothing compared to me. NOTHING!"

Ulani. That must have been it. Her father had a new mistress who was beautiful and kind. She'd given Belladonna a baked pastry she'd made herself. Had brushed her hair and held her against her chest while Belladonna cried softly. How did her mother know, though?

"Tell me what you said to her." Cassava bit out the words and with each one she slapped Belladonna again.

"I said nothing, nothing! She gave me a pastry. I didn't even like it." That wasn't the truth, though; it had tasted of strawberries, Belladonna's favorite. And Ulani had made it for her, made it special for her.

"Who braided your hair then?" The words were deadly soft and Belladonna knew what was coming, knew she'd been caught in a lie. She tried to back away. Her six years on the planet had taught her the mood swings of her mother, and that lying was her only hope of avoiding a beating. Even if she got caught, it could be the only chance she had of surviving. "Not Ulani, she didn't do it."

"You little liar."

The blows went on and on, raining down like a thunderstorm that seemed to never end. The pain lanced through her, and at one point she wondered if this time she wouldn't wake up. That would be good. To just go to sleep and not hurt anymore. The mother goddess would be kind. At least, she hoped she would be. Maybe the mother goddess looked like Ulani. Yes, she could imagine that easily.

As suddenly as it started, the beating was over and Belladonna lay on the floor, shivering and aching. Hurting in both body and heart. Alone. Scared. Night fell and she crawled into a corner, taking the tiny blanket she loved so much with her. Blue and green, stitched with her namesake, she lay down on it.

"Mama," she whispered. "Mama, why don't you love me?"

I jerked hard out of the memory unable to stomach yet another truth of our family. I fell away from Belladonna and vomited all over the ground. Burying my fingers into the hot sand, I struggled to breath around the sobs that built in my chest. Sorrow and pity flooded me. Just a little girl, she'd been so tiny, so afraid. The sorrow and pity were gone in a flash, wiped away in a flush of anger so intense I couldn't see straight.

This had been going on for so many years and the mother goddess had done nothing. Nothing but let the smallest of her children suffer. I drove my power deep into the earth, the fury I felt akin to when I'd lost Bramley. "You let them be hurt. You LET THEM!" I screamed the words, didn't even think about the pain that would hit me when I grabbed for my power. The ground shook with a violence that bucked the whole island, sending the ocean away from the shore in a rush that left fish flopping on the wet sand.

"ANSWER ME! WHY?" I couldn't contain it, the rage, the pain, the loss. Belladonna was a creature of her mother's creation. But she'd been a child once. A child who'd needed and deserved love and protection. Yet she'd been left to her mother's mercy which was anything but.

"Lark, have you lost your mind?" Belladonna screamed at me, grabbing my arms, dragging me up the beach. "The water is coming back."

I let go of the earth's power and spun around. The ocean was rushing toward us. I'd inadvertently caused a tsunami. We ran, Belladonna tripping and falling over her dress. I scooped her up over my shoulder and bolted for high ground. She bounced and screamed from her perch. "Hurry!"

All my training came together in a split second. I knew I could outrun the water on my own, but not carrying Belladonna and her dress. She was going to have to help. "Pull the ground up, block the water!"

"I can't, I can't feel the earth!"

What the hell was going on? There was no way I could carry her and try to reach the earth's power. I dropped my sister, and faced the oncoming water. I pushed past the fear of the pain, reached for the power beneath our feet and felt . . . nothing.

You have no right to chastise me, Larkspur. The mother goddess spoke to me, her voice firm and calm. Apologize and I will allow you access to the earth again.

I couldn't do it. My anger was too new, too raw.

With a snarl, I grabbed Belladonna around the waist. "Hold on."

"Are you serious?" She screeched as the wave swallowed us whole. For just a moment we floated in a stillness that seemed peaceful before we were thrown forward, farther up the beach. The water was murky and I struggled to see through the churned up sand and plant life. We brushed against the top of a tree and I grabbed hold of the branches. Belladonna clung to me like a monkey and at first, I thought we were going to make it.

Then the wave began to recede, the water pulling on us with the force of an entire ocean behind it. Belladonna slipped, her grip nowhere near as strong as mine. Letting go of the tree with one hand, I grabbed a handful of her hair and buried my fingers in deep. She might have a few less strands when we were done, but I couldn't lose her to the water.

Not when I was the cause of the tsunami in the first place.

The ocean dropped around us, our bodies slowly lowering until we were standing on firm ground. So to speak. The branches of the tree tangled around us. Below me, Belladonna gave a groan. "Let go of my hair, Lark."

"You'll fall," I pointed out.

"LET GO OF MY HAIR!" she screeched. I did as I was told and opened my fingers.

She tumbled down through the tree, her dress tearing more than once before she hit the ground below with a thick thud.

I shimmied down, dropping beside her. Carefully, I put a hand on her back, her body shivering under my fingers. "Belladonna, are you okay?"

She slapped my hands away. "What the hell is wrong with you? What are you trying to do, show me up?"

"No, of course not."

What was she talking about anyway? It wasn't like there was anyone to see what had just happened except her and me.

"I'm telling Father about this the second we get home."

I let out a sigh. "I would expect nothing less from you."

Her eyes shot to mine and for just a second I saw the little girl I'd experienced through her memories.

"Mama, why don't you love me?"

Shaking my head, I held a hand out to her. She let me help her to her feet at least.

"I need a new dress. This one is ruined. Which is fine by me, I hated it anyway."

"I can fix it," I pulled a dagger from a strap on my calf.

"What are you doing? Lark, stop it!" But I'd already cut the train off the bottom and sliced through some of the thick material leaving the bottom edge jagged. With tiny cuts, I split the material and then pulled each slit apart. The full skirt became a loose, many pieced hula type dress. Belladonna shifted her feet and the tiny slices moved around baring bits and pieces of her smooth legs.

"That's actually not bad." She patted me on the top of my head absently. As if I were a servant. Did she know what I'd seen of her memory? Probably not. The only reason Ash had known what I'd seen of his the first time I'd Traveled was that he'd known it was a possibility. My mother, Ulani, had the same ability. Or curse, depending how you looked at it.

"Let's find a boat." I stared past her to the devastation that had occurred. How the hell were we going to find a boat with this mess? Trees were down, human garbage was everywhere and—

"Will that work?" Belladonna pointed toward the water's edge. A rowboat floated, oars sitting balanced across the middle. As if that were a normal occurrence immediately after a tsunami.

"There's no way that just showed up," I said, pulling my spear from my side. With a swift twist, I connected the two pieces and held the weapon out in front of me as I approached the bobbing boat.

"The Undine's must have sent it. Maybe their civil war is over? That would be brilliant. I'd rather not go and deal with the fish lips." Belladonna leaned forward, her feet dipping into the water; I pushed her back.

"Stay behind me. We don't know this isn't a trap."

Surprisingly, she nodded and let me go first. I stepped into the water waiting for something to grab me and pull me under. My experience with the other two families, air and fire, had not been . . . pleasant.

Funny enough, I didn't expect my visit to the Undines to be any different.

I used the hook on my spear to pull the boat closer. Nothing pulled back or launched out at us. The boated floated nicely toward me, bobbing on the water almost as if welcoming us with a tiny dance.

Dragging it onto dry land, I looked it over. A simple slatted wooden boat with oars, two seats—one for the rower in the center, and one for the person being ferried at the prow. There was no question where I'd be sitting. On the center seat was a thick envelope with no writing on it. Belladonna grabbed it before I could and peeled it open. A slow smile slid across her face. "We are cordially invited to come to the Deep. Courtesy of Requiem."

"Do you know him?" I took the paper from her and looked it over. Nothing else. No clues.

"He's one of the men vying for the throne."

"Then do we really want his help? Aren't we supposed to be neutral in this?"

She let out an exasperated sigh and shook the paper at me, and then at the boat. "Larkspur, how do you expect we're going to get to the Deep without a boat? Just because we take this rickety little thing doesn't mean we are on Requiem's side."

It was my turn to snort. "That is not how politics work, and we both know it."

But she had a point. We needed to get to the Deep, and right now I wasn't sure we'd find a better way.

"Come on, let's get this show on the road. Not that there's

really a road, but definitely a show." I helped her in then shoved the boat out, wading up to my waist before pulling myself in. I slid the oars into the round oar locks and drove the paddles down. The water swirled out around the oars each time I dipped them, eddies disappearing into the crystal-clear water. Belladonna leaned off the side of the boat, trailing a hand in the ripples from the boat cutting the water. "You know, this is really nice."

"Easy for you to say," I grunted as I adjusted our direction. From the globe, I knew I had to head straight east from the coast of Bermuda. Sweat already coursed down my spine and arms. The heat was unreal and the humidity high, and I knew it wouldn't take me long to run out of energy at that rate.

We were in the open ocean within an hour, far enough out that I could barely see the island we'd started on. I sighted it once more, checked our bearings, and continued to row east.

I eyed up my sister, lounging in her seat. "So do you have a plan to get the information Father wants?"

Belladonna sniffed and raised her hands to her hair. With deft fingers she twisted her long locks off her neck and into a perfect French roll. "Men spill their secrets when they are in bed. Even you have to know that."

My stomach tightened and I stopped rowing. "Father sent you here to sleep with someone?"

She turned on the wooden seat to look me in the eye. "You still think he's a good man, don't you? Even after the way he's treated you, and don't give me that look. We all see it. He treats you like compost, Lark. The king will use the tools he has at hand. You. Me. Ash. Whoever he has to in order to rule. That's politics, but of course, what would you know of politics, grubbing in the dirt for most of your life." She flipped a stray curl of hair over her shoulder, and quite literally looked down her nose at me.

I leaned forward and the boat rocked under my shift in weight. She let out a squeak and grabbed the edge of her seat, effectively pinning her where she was. One way or another I was going to get through to her.

"I understand all too clearly the politics. Those in power make the rules and those rules change as it suits their wishes and whims. I know Father has made mistakes and worm shit choices. But you and I? We have to decide whose example we follow. And as far as I can see, you are still far too much your mother's daughter and I hate it. I hate that you think you can't get information without spreading your legs like a common whore. Has it never occurred to you to use your brain instead of your body?"

Her gray eyes narrowed. "You are blind, Lark. Blind. You assume you know me, but you don't. It takes nothing to get a man to believe he will bed you. A soft touch. A whisper. That doesn't mean you actually go through with it."

I sat back, blinking. "You mean you tease them?"

"Unlike *your* mother, I am not a whore. And I certainly wouldn't be sleeping with anyone within any of the other families. Can you imagine the horror?"

Of course not. I let out a bitter laugh at the thought. "Your mother would kill you herself if she thought you carried a half-breed child."

Belladonna turned her face away from me to look across the water, an icy chill rolling off her. "Get rowing, Ender. I want to be in the Deep before the end of the day."

A part of me wanted to grab and shake her. I was close to pushing her to look into a mirror she'd been avoiding. Her memory I'd seen was at the front of my brain and I saw so clearly the child she had been; the little girl who wanted so desperately to be loved.

I wanted to save her, as I hadn't been able to save Bram. Yes, she was older now, but that didn't mean Cassava wasn't still using her. Hurting her with lies and manipulation only I could see.

She shifted so she could look at me. Raising an eyebrow, she waved at the oars. "Are we going? No, we aren't. Do your job, Ender. Stop thinking you have the brains to be an ambassador."

With what felt like a momentous effort, I kept my mouth shut. What did I think, that Belladonna and I were suddenly becoming best friends on this trip? Maybe a part of me had hoped.

Belladonna snapped her fingers. "Your only job is to keep me safe."

I put my hands on the oars and drove them into the water. "That it is, Ambassador. That it is."

Chapter 5

Night fell as I rowed, the sky deepening to a black, broken only by the stars. "No moon tonight," I said as I took a break, massaging my arms and hands. Hours of rowing and still no welcome into the Deep other than the note left on the boat for us.

"Does that matter?"

I rolled my shoulders and stretched my arms over my head to ease the ache in my muscles through my back. "Maybe. Awfully hard to see if someone is coming up on us if the dark hides them."

Belladonna let out a little squeak. "What are you talking about?"

"I don't want to scare you." That was the truth. Ash had been very clear we might end up on the receiving end of some unhappy Undines.

"Tell me what you're talking about!" The demand shouldn't

have been unexpected, but for the last few hours I'd experienced a strange sensation of closeness with my older sister. Maybe it was just because she'd been so quiet and I could pretend we were getting along.

Taking up the rowing again, I chose my words carefully. "The civil war has left all the ambassadors dead. And while we had a nice little welcome note on the boat, I am not convinced this might not be a trap."

"And you are just telling me this now?" Belladonna reached across as if to slap me and the boat rocked precariously.

"Belladonna, stop! You'll tip us into the water." I put my hands on the sides of the boat, forcing it to settle down. "The Undines might still let us in. We may be able to help where no one else could because you are a princess. That is what Father is banking on. That you will be safe." I chose not to mention he also needed me out of the way while the ambassador from the Pit roamed our home. Then again, that thought of treachery swam through my brain. We could very well be handed over to the Undines and Father would be rid of two very prickly problems. It was one of those moments I wondered on our two names. Both plants we were named for were beautiful . . . and poisonous.

"Belladonna, listen to me. The only way we are going to survive this is if we work together. Understand?"

Her body went still as she stared out. "Lark, I think I see something."

I grabbed the left oar and dragged it through the water, spinning us sideways. Three triangular fins cut through the liquid darkness. The only thing giving them away was the tiny waves rolling around them.

"Belladonna, don't move."

But I was too late and she was too afraid, or at least, that was what I thought. My sister spun on her seat. "Ender, you have to protect me."

I was going to tell her that was my job. But a bump under the boat rocked us hard to the right. The water lapped at the edge, and splashed in. I caught a glimpse of movement slicing through the water, the flip of a tail, the quick glisten of rows of teeth. Belladonna screamed and clutched the high side of the boat, which of course just sent us swinging back the other way with a force that flipped the boat completely.

Eyes open, the salt water stung as I submerged under the water, but I wasn't going down with my eyes clamped shut. The boat still floated above us, how in the mother goddess's name it had stayed upright was beyond me, but I would count it a blessing.

I pushed to the surface and something bumped against my left leg. Okay, not something, I knew what it was; I just chose not to think about it and the teeth attached. "Not happening, my friend." I grabbed the edge of the boat and hauled myself in. Six inches of water had the boat riding low, but it was afloat and that was all that mattered.

"Lark!" Belladonna screamed my name and I twisted to see her being circled by two fins. I drove the oars into the water and rowed to her. The golden strands of her dress floated out around her, and I watched in horror as one of the sharks opened its mouth and clamped down on the material. Belladonna's eyes met mine and I reached for her as the shark jerked its head back and forth, sawing through the material, yanking her around like rag doll.

"Please, don't let me die," Belladonna screamed, her hands tightening on mine.

"I won't, just hang on to me."

Please let that not be a lie. I pulled her toward the boat. How was the shark not through the damn dress already? Understanding and horror hit me at the same time. There was only one answer. My hands slipped on her arms as the shark pulled her down, her lips touching the surface of the water.

"Belladonna, has it got your leg?"

She nodded, her head rolling to one side as she passed out.

"Bella, hang on." Her childhood nickname flowed from my lips at the thought of losing her. I had to let go of her with one hand in order to reach my spear, still hooked into the bottom of the boat. I whipped it out, spinning it through the air.

Growling with the effort, I pulled Belladonna and subsequently the shark closer. Close enough to use my spear. I thrust it into the water and the shark's flesh. The tip drove in deep, the razor sharp edges cutting through the thick hide as if it were paper. The pull on Belladonna eased and I hauled her into the boat. Moving fast, I laid her on the bottom of the boat and lifted her leg, propping it on the middle seat.

The calf muscle was still there, but it was torn to hell, tiny shreds of skin flapping every time she even twitched and the blood flow was slowing which was a bad sign. It should have been spurting, the arterial pulse sending it out in jets. I ripped off the bottom half of her dress and wrapped it around the leg as tightly as I could, then lifted her whole leg, resting it on my shoulder. "Belladonna, I need you to wake up."

Nothing, she didn't even flutter her eyelids. The blood no longer poured from her leg, but I knew if I didn't do something she was going to die no matter what I'd promised. Time to lay it all on the line.

I stood as the boat was hammered from bellow, the hull creaking and cracking under the impact. "Undine, call off your familiars or the heir of the Earth Elementals will die and the king's wrath will know no bounds." My words echoed across the water, but there was no response.

Spear in my hand, I stared into the water and waited for the right moment. To kill another elemental's familiar was a bad, bad thing. Not quite as bad as killing another elemental, but close.

"You will force me to kill your pets!" I raised my arm, muscles tensed, and I let out the breath I'd been holding. The boat was slammed hard on the right side and I spun to see the gaping mouth of a Mako shark snapping at the edge of Belladonna's good leg. With a back swing I ripped the blade of my spear through the tip of the shark's nose, cutting it completely off. Blood spurted out and the shark slid back into the water, thrashing and stirring up a foam of salt water and blood.

Belladonna let out a groan. "Lark, I'm dying."

"No, you aren't."

"Don't lie to me, I see the mother goddess. She's calling to me. She looks like your mother. I'm sorry I called her a whore."

"That's nice. Wave goodbye to her and keep your ass awake." I raised my hand over my head. "Undines, you will let us into the Deep and heal her or we will raze your civil war-ridden city to the depths!"

Panic made me reach for the earth again, but the power slid through me. If I could just grab hold of it, maybe I could cause another tsunami. I could force the Undines to let us in. But only if I could convince the mother goddess I was contrite. "I'm sorry I yelled before," I cried out to the mother goddess.

There was no answer and I knew there was something the mother goddess wanted, there had to be. "Please, Mother, you said I am your chosen one, help me!"

Swear your life to me.

I didn't question what she was asking, or how it might impact my decisions. "I swear my life to you!"

A sense of satisfaction flowed around me that was not my own. I'd pleased the mother goddess.

Child, you are forgiven. But you must realize there is a reason for everything. And you will not know the meaning for most, nor are you meant to. Accept and obey me. You are my chosen. Now, save your sister.

I grabbed hold of the power, my fear making it hard to focus, but the anger sustained me. Now what did I do, though? We were in the middle of the ocean, with no land in sight.

Belladonna was going to die, and I could do nothing about it.

The boat rocked again and Belladonna let out another moan. But it wasn't the sharks moving us.

The waves around us shifted, rolling as if something below pushed. A deep, steady rumble shook the tiny vessel, but I held my stance. Death was not something I truly feared, not after everything I'd seen. My mother would welcome me with open arms on the other side of the veil. I would hold my baby brother again. But Belladonna . . . I couldn't let her die without a fight, no matter the things she'd done.

Even if the mother goddess hadn't told me to save her, I would fight for her life.

The thundering of wind and a massive pressure change in the air like an incoming storm roared toward us, and the water swelled. Our boat was propelled forward with a speed I could never match rowing. I crouched and cradled Belladonna to my chest. "They're taking us in. We'll get you to a healer." Again, I could only hope I was not feeding her a lie. I really had no idea what was going on, but good or ill, we were about to find out.

The water shifted again and a mist rose, hiding us. I could see nothing ahead, nothing below. The fog grew so thick I barely could make out the lines of Belladonna's face even though my head was tucked next to hers.

This was the fog that hid the Deep, and we were going through it.

Evaporating as quickly as it appeared, the mist was gone and all around, spires shot up through the water, glistening, lit from within. I counted seven that rivaled our Spiral for size on the exterior. Made up of coral and glass, the Deep glittered like diamonds.

Even with Belladonna's life hanging on the line, I couldn't help but stare at the beauty that unfolded. Ornate fountains rising thirty feet into the air pulsed with water and tiny fish that jumped and leapt as they cascaded into the wading pools lit with glowing phosphorescence. Brilliantly colored reefs made up the lower portion of the city. Pinks, blues, greens, and purples blended into one another. Though the lower buildings closest to the water were humble and simply made, the main portion of the island was built in a circular manner, tiered spirals reaching hundreds of feet into the sky. Each spiral glittered as though sprinkled with glittering jewels.

Our tiny boat drove through the waterway in the center of the city, stopping against a dock. A tall, whip-lean man waited for us. A man I knew and almost trusted.

When I'd met him, he'd been kind, and I could only hope that kindness was not false. He reached down and helped me out as I held

Belladonna to my chest. "I recognized your voice, Lark. Otherwise, we would not have let you in."

"No time for niceties. Someone's pet took a chunk out of her leg."

He nodded, his face grim. "Dark times, Lark. You have chosen to visit in very dark times." Dolph led the way up the dock and through an archway that took us deeper into the city. "What are you doing here, Lark?"

"I'm here as the Ender for our ambassador and princess, Belladonna." I didn't want to say too much. I didn't know if I could trust Dolph. I wanted to. He had taught me in the few short months I'd trained to become an Ender. But now he was on the other side of a divide from me—an Ender I might have to face in order to protect my charge.

I felt like I was playing a game with rules I didn't know. Or maybe there were no rules.

Dolph didn't ask any more questions, and a minute later, we pushed through a set of doors that led into the healers' room.

The healers rushed forward, not caring we weren't from their family. That was the beauty of a healer—they wanted to help, regardless of the family or race. I let them take Belladonna and lay her on a bed. Her blood splashed across the white sheets; a shot of color that stood out in a brilliant spray.

"We can wait outside. The healers will take care of her," Dolph said quietly.

I shook him off. "No. I will wait here." I swung my spear point down and leaned against it. "Thank you, Dolph. She would have died."

His turquoise eyes met mine. "I know. That was the plan. Be wary, Ender Larkspur. You and your charge are most certainly not welcome here, no matter what you were told."

I snorted softly as he left, and pulled the note out of my vest. Requiem wanted us here. Whoever he was. I crumpled it in my hand. Games of life and death, moves and countermoves, and goddess-bedamned politics. This was not my world, and I hated trying to navigate it. As I stood there, a sudden gratitude flowed through me for my upbringing. If I'd grown up in the Spiral with my siblings, I wouldn't have been trained for this; perhaps it was a blessing wrapped in hardship I hadn't seen. Sort of exactly what the mother goddess said not long ago.

Belladonna moaned on the table as the healers worked on her leg. They pieced it together quickly, and it hit me that the speed at which they worked spoke of dealing with shark bites on a regular basis.

One of the healers, a woman with the same green-tinged hair and webbed hands as Dolph, came to me. She was a little shorter than my six feet, but not by much. "Your ambassador will be fine, and now we must insist you go. She will be safe here."

"I'm sorry, I didn't catch your name." I stared her down and waited while she struggled to pull herself together. My eyes, one gold, one green, disturbed people. They marked me as "other," and "other" was not respected in our world.

"Ayu."

"Well, Ayu, until my ambassador releases me to leave, I'm not moving from this spot." I smiled at her, but I knew I was swimming in dangerous waters. Ayu's eyes narrowed and two spots of bright purple bloomed high on her cheeks.

"I am the First Healer. Do you dare doubt my word?"

I continued to smile, though my words were anything but pleasant. "We were just attacked by someone's familiars after being welcomed to the Deep. Forgive me if I don't trust you."

Her body jerked as if I'd slapped her. "Someone welcomed you?"

I shoved the crumpled note at her. She took it, smoothed it out, and I watched her carefully. Her eyes widened and her mouth dropped as she read. Good sign? I didn't think so.

"Where is he? I'd like to speak with him about his welcome."

"He . . ." Her eyes lifted and then looked past me, widening farther. I spun, spear swirling in front of me, stopping at the throat of a beefy looking Undine. Unlike the whip-thin Dolph, the man behind me rippled with muscles and had a mouth full of teeth that grinned at me. His eyes, though, were jet black, not unlike those of the sharks we'd faced a short time past. He slid into the room, avoiding my blade.

"Ah, cousin, please. You can put your weapon away."

I didn't lower the spear, despite his invocation of the familiar 'cousin.' All elementals thought of each other as distant branches of the same family. And just like most families, we didn't always get along. I stepped sideways, blocking him from getting to Bella. "I think I'll keep it out until you tell me who you are and why you set your familiars on us."

The room went quiet except for the soft moan of my sister on the table.

He spread his hands. "My familiars have minds of their own, as they all do. You would know that if you had one yourself."

I glared at him. The insult was subtle. I wasn't strong enough to have been given a familiar. The more familiars an elemental had, the stronger they were. We'd had three sharks trying to take us down.

Which meant this one was going to be a problem.

"I don't care if you have a dozen sharks, you should be able to control your familiars."

His grin widened and the resemblance between him and his familiars deepened. Yeah, this guy was not cool. "My name is Requiem. And I am about to be crowned the King of the Deep. A bastard, I'll admit, but that doesn't make me any less of an heir to the throne, does it . . . Larkspur?"

While I didn't lower the tip of my spear, my mind reeled from the information, and the fact he knew me and my status. "You welcome us here, then try to kill us?"

"Your ambassador put on quite a power show causing the tsunami. How do I know she isn't here to wipe us all out? I have to protect my people. The best way to do that is for you to put yourself into danger. Which you did quite nicely, by the way."

He thought Belladonna had caused the earthquake. That was probably for the best; if they thought she was powerful, they would be more careful with her. We slowly shifted around the room, mirroring each other's steps as he tried to get an open shot past me. "You aren't getting any closer to her and you didn't answer my question. Why welcome then try to kill us?"

"A woman with that kind of power should not be allowed to roam without someone holding her reins." He slid his hand down and grabbed his crotch.

"Sea slime," Ayu whispered behind me.

I had to agree.

Requiem paced closer to me, and I could feel the rest of the room shift back. They were afraid of him, the tension rising with each step he took. He reached out and touched the healer closest to him, running his hand down her neck to cup her breast, squeezing the nipple. "These are my people. I will do what I wish here."

I didn't back down, just shifted my stance and thrust my spear around to point not at his belly, or even his neck. I tucked it up between his legs with a swift flick of my wrist, pressing it through the material of his pants. He dropped his hand from the healer and she scuttled away, well out of his reach. His eyes dropped to the spear tip and then rose to my face. "You are a brassy one, aren't you?"

"You have no idea, but I do believe you and I aren't done," I said. "Get out of here. You're bothering the healers."

"You can't protect them all, and certainly not them and your ambassador. Who will you choose? I'm so very glad you are here, Larkspur. I've been bored, and I do believe I'm looking forward to playing with you and your ambassador." He stepped back, his hands spread wide. "Welcome, little Terraling, welcome to the Deep."

Chapter 6

After the show Requiem and I put on, the healers seemed more than happy to have me stay. Ayu brought me a steaming hot drink that was salty and sweet, and I gulped it down, pausing only for a moment to nod and say, "Thank you."

"The least we can do. No one stands up to him, Ender. That you did, that is worthy of respect and a hot drink." She gave me a wink, but the lines etched around her eyes showed how much strain she was under.

I looked over my shoulder, for a minute forgetting that "Ender" was my title now. "He is the bastard son of the king who died?"

"Yes, though there are rumors about how the king died—"

"Ayu, hush, you'll get us killed, or worse, banished!" Another of the healers spoke in undertones as she tended Belladonna. We were the only ones in the infirmary, but still they all acted like other elementals listened in. Maybe they were. Ayu shook her head, her hair bound up with sea kelp and dotted with tiny starfish that danced lightly as she moved.

"It is common knowledge. The king was healthy, robust, and well loved. He went to bed one night and didn't wake the next morning. His body was shriveled as though he were a thousand years dead, not a few hours." Her eyes filled with tears. "Requiem took over immediately, citing the Deep could not wait for the heir to come of age."

I downed the last of my drink and let out a slow breath. "And there is no one who could stand against him? The proper heir is too weak?"

Ayu shook her head. "I have said enough. Drink and flee. You do not want to be on the receiving end of Requiem's games."

With Belladonna out cold, I needed to move fast and Ayu's advice was good. The quicker we got the information we needed and left, the better. "We were sent to observe, to find out who our king should back if it came to a full out war."

Ayu shook her head slowly. "There is no real choice, and there will be no war. Requiem has only to wait until his sister dies and then he will have the throne."

I frowned into my empty cup. "His sister is sick? Why is she not here with you then?"

All three healers turned away. I grabbed Ayu before she could move from me. "Tell me."

She jerked out of my hand. "No. It is forbidden. Requiem will soon be the king and we must learn to live with his rules no matter how we may hate it."

Worm shit and green sticks, this was turning out to be more of a mess than even Ash and my father thought. "And the other ambassadors? They were killed by Requiem?"

The other two healers left the room tripping over themselves and each other to get away. Leaving just me, Ayu, and Belladonna. Ayu wiped a hand over her face. "Get away, Ender. Take your ambassador and get out of here as quickly as you can. Do you understand me?"

I nodded; she was right. The visit had been anything but sweet, but I was going to keep it short. "Is she well enough to travel?"

"No, but she won't die. The wound is stitched together and will take time to heal. Take her, go. And . . . thank you for trying to protect us. Even our own Enders won't face him now."

Chills swept through me as Ayu left through a door in the back of the room, the soft click of the latch closing the only sound. I strode to my sister. "Bella, wake up, it's time to go."

"Lark, I just want to sleep. Leave me alone." She flung an arm over her eyes. I grabbed a sheet and wrapped it around her.

"Be quiet. We're leaving, right now." I leaned in and scooped her up into my arms, doing my best not to jostle her leg. Still, she moaned and bit her lip, tears tracing down her cheeks. Eyes fluttering open, the gray of the iris dark with pain, she stared up at me. "You didn't let me die."

"Why would I do that?" I didn't look at her as I peered out the doorway. I'd not paid attention to the direction we'd come. I'd been too damned concerned with Bella.

"Because I'm an awful person. Because I *am* my mother's daughter."

I did glance down at her then. "No, you're not. You're my sister and no matter what, I will always look out for you. And I choose to believe you would do the same for me."

She sobbed against my chest. "Lark, I'm so sorry." The adrenaline rush that came with being injured was leaving her, which only gave way to more tears and blubbering words.

"Shut it. Right now, we have to find our way out." I stumbled through the hallways until I made it to an open courtyard. A waterway ran on my left, boats bobbing in the dark of the night.

I looked down a cobbled road, eyeing up the route. The sound of waves against rocks drew me to the left. I would follow the waterway back to the docks; that would be the best way. Belladonna wasn't heavy, but she was a solid girl, and as we walked the fatigue of the day caught up to me. The explosion of my power into the earth, the rowing, the fight with the sharks, and now this—I had taken three wrong turns and had to backtrack, only increasing how long it was taking. My arms shook as I struggled to keep her from tumbling to the pebbled road. I leaned against a wall, breathing hard. "Bella, listen to me. I'm going to put you down. Then I'm going to run and see which direction we need to take. I'll come back for you, just don't move. Okay?" I helped her sit between two buildings. Her gray eyes filled with pain and yet I could see the trust in them.

"Lark, we don't know anything yet!"

I grabbed her face and forced her to look at me. "They tried to kill us both, Belladonna. Would you stay and let them succeed? Requiem is running the show here, and there is nothing we can do about that. I am in charge of your safety and I say it's time to go."

"What about the Pit? Fiametta will take you."

So she knew about that. I let her go and rubbed a hand over my face. "Your life before mine, Ambassador."

Her eyes widened and she slowly nodded. "Be careful," she whispered. I stood and sprinted from her. Without the burden of her body weighing me down, I could find our way out. Four quick turns, a dash across an open courtyard, and I was at the docks. No one was moving around outside of their homes, which should have been a good thing. But all I could think was why the hell wasn't there a single person out and about. It was dark, but not late, surely not past midnight.

Scurrying forward, keeping low to the ground, I reached our boat. Loosening the knots that held it tightly to the shore, I made sure the oars were set up and ready. Satisfied I'd prepped it as much as I could, I bolted back the way I'd come. Across the courtyard, turning right, left, left.

Belladonna was not where I'd put her. "Bella," I whispered as loud as I dared. I searched the ground where I'd sat her down, and my body grew cold with a certainty. There was no blood trail, which meant she hadn't gotten up and walked away.

Someone had picked her up and carried her. The scuff of a foot on the stone was the only warning I had. Spinning, I had my spear pointed out as I stepped into the thrust—I saw Dolph's wide eyes at the last second. I turned my wrist and the blade cut through the air an inch away from slicing through his skull.

I pulled myself up, but didn't put my weapon away. "Where is she?"

"Requiem has her. And he requests that you attend them."

"Tell me you don't follow him." I couldn't believe it of Dolph. For the little I knew him, I had a hard time seeing him side with Requiem. Dolph seemed so level headed. So . . . good.

"We all do what we must. But if it makes you feel better, I side with Finley. She is the king's legitimate daughter." Dolph crooked a finger and I had no choice but to follow him. Finley . . . so that was the other heir to the throne—the rightful heir.

Once more, Dolph led me around the maze of buildings, over two low arched bridges. and finally into an open coliseum. Circular and tiered, opened to the night sky, it was full of Undines. That explained why there was no one at the docks. Around us the spires rose high into the sky. The tallest stood as sentinels farthest away, bridges glittering between them. Another set of spires encircled, closer and shorter than the others, and a third set even closer loomed above. Undines hung from windows in the closest spires, staring down at us.

I caught a glimpse of Ayu in the stands closest to the circular coliseum—saw her eyes as she looked away. Pity and sorrow had been heavy in that one glance. Not really a good sign, and not something I chose to dwell on.

Ahead of me, Requiem stood at a podium a foot above the main floor. Belladonna was beside him, shaking and trembling. Her wound had broken open, but it wasn't gushing. Her face was pale though and the way her eyes glossed over I knew she was close to passing out.

"Larkspur, how nice of you to join us. Your ambassador here is in no shape to fight, which is a pity, considering her show of power on the beach. But as it is, we need you two to prove you are strong enough to stay here. You will fight for your ambassador. A proxy. You lose, we kill her and throw your bodies into the ocean. You win, and you may stay as our guests as long as I wish."

As long as he wished? That was not a good sign, but I doubted we would actually have a choice when it came down to it.

Dolph jerked as if he'd been shot with a bolt from a crossbow. His voice was low and I doubted anyone but me could hear him. "He will never let you leave alive, Lark. You have to fight his champion. Mako."

"A fight, I can handle."

Dolph grabbed my arm, his fingers digging into my bicep as he dragged me around to face him. "You will be in water up to your waist. To win you must drown your opponent. This is a very old tradition Requiem has brought forward. With his sister out of the picture, there is no one to stop him."

I swallowed the fear that curled up my throat and tried to choke me. Across from us, a tightly muscled Undine stepped out from behind Requiem and Bella. He was a little shorter than me, but by the way he moved, he was all muscle. His shirt gaped at the belly giving a glimpse of a torso that seemed chiseled of pale blue stone. His eyes and hair matched the color of his skin. He looked like he'd been frozen and then thawed. Webbed hands and the slight flutter of gills just below his ears completed the package. His eyes never stopped moving, watching everything and nothing all at once.

"Is he an Ender?"

"No, he's a killer."

Startled, I looked to Dolph. "What?"

"Pulled from the cells to be Requiem's personal fighter. He was the last serial killer we put away, almost a hundred years ago. He is mad, Lark. Mad and violent beyond reason. He has killed every challenger sent forward."

"Enders?"

"Yes."

I licked my lips, fear climbing my throat for a second time, and then I shrugged. There was little choice here, which meant I faced Mako no matter how afraid I was. I spun my spear out, pointing at Requiem. "What are the rules, if any?"

Requiem let out a long low laugh, but the crowd didn't laugh with him. "There are only three rules, Ender. First. Kill or be killed. There will be no ties."

Mako swayed where he stood, hands flexing. I looked at Bella. She would die if I failed, and once more, I would be the one who had fallen at the finish line. Requiem held up his hand. "Second. No weapons allowed. This is strength of body only. And third, no power of the earth or water may be used. Dolph, prepare her for the Depths."

Behind me, Dolph let out a soft groan, he spun me to face him and as his hands stripped me of my weapons, he spoke in a low whisper. "Lark, I will create a diversion, and you will run. No one will stop you. I can't save you both but you can get away."

I put a hand on his shoulder. "I'm not leaving her."

"You can't beat him." Dolph grabbed my arms. "He's a survivor of the cells and has killed a dozen Enders already."

"He's not the only survivor standing in front of you, Dolph." I pushed away from him and faced Requiem once more, a strange calm flowing over my body. I might die, but I would not do so without a knock-down, drag-out fight. Spreading my arms wide I turned a slow circle. "I have no weapons other than my hands. And now you will swear that my sister and I will go free when I kill your champion."

The crowd gave a low murmur and Requiem laughed and gave me a mocking bow. "On the redemption of my soul, on being denied the grace of the Mother's last embrace, I swear that if you defeat my champion, you and your sister will be honored guests for the remainder of your stay." His black eyes glittered as he watched me. Not exactly what I'd asked for, but I would take it.

"Not *if* I defeat him. When." I rolled my shoulders and the ground beneath my feet rumbled. The center of the coliseum where Mako and I stood lowered. Dolph stepped out of the center and moved to a seat along the tiers. Within seconds, I was staring up at the crowd. Mako and I had been dropped into a pit twice my height, and four times as wide that was quickly filling with water. Just below my waist, the flow stopped rising; deep enough to make someone think they could survive, but too deep to have any real range of motion. This was going to suck.

Mako circled toward me, cutting through the water like his namesake.

"Let it begin!" Requiem roared above us, and the Undines gave a weak cheer. Obviously, they weren't any happier about this than I was.

Mako splashed water at me, spraying my face. "Little Ender, you are too pretty. After I kill you, I'll ask for your body."

I curled my lips, tasted the salt water, but didn't take my eyes from him. Nor did I answer. The water pulled at me, slowing my movements to the point I wasn't sure how the hell I was going to—

Mako struck, his foot slicing through the water and slamming into my thigh. I sloshed in the water as I stumbled backward. He grinned at me. "Pretty little starfish . . . I'm going to lick your cold, dead titties."

Okay, that was disgusting, and I wasn't letting him push me around with words or fists. I stopped moving. "Come then, you twisted, tiny man. It's obvious you can't get laid unless the woman is dead."

He nodded with such violence that his teeth clacked together. "Dead is better. No nagging."

Above us, Requiem roared with laughter. "That is the truth, my friends. Dead women don't nag."

Mako slid through the water toward me and I held my ground. I had a couple of inches of height on Mako and I had to use it to my advantage. He came within range of my reach, then closer.

"You aren't afraid of me, why not?" He circled me and I moved with him, waiting for the perfect moment.

"I don't fear death."

He dropped into the water. Just his eyes peered up at me. He swam a circle, spitting water like a fountain through his two front teeth. Like this was a game.

Of course, to him it probably was.

Above us, the crowd was silent. I didn't dare glance up.

"Mako, show her your teeth, man!" Requiem called out.

Mako dove under the water and kicked toward me with his mouth open wide. I jumped straight into the air and when I came down, I landed on his back, pressing him to the bottom. He twisted, throwing me off with ease and I went under.

Fighting panic, I pushed off, flailing to get to the surface.

I stood, water dripping off me to the sound of laughter. Mako and Requiem were howling.

"Oh, pretty starfish, you should see your face." Mako grinned at me. "That was just the start, wait 'til you're breathing the water and I'm riding your body and tasting your blood." He strode toward me, splashing water. A game.

A game he thought there was no way he could lose.

And if he believed I was weak . . . that might help me. I stumbled back and held out a hand. "You stay there, don't come any closer."

Laughing, he grabbed my wrist and I gave token resistance. "Let me go."

"You can do better than that," he licked his lips and then blew me a kiss as he began to draw me toward him.

Again, I fought, but not enough to throw him off. Not enough to tip my hand.

He let me go and I tumbled back into the wall with a hard thump, slumped, and cringed against the wall.

From above us came a heavy, drawn out sigh. "Enough, Mako. She obviously isn't a fighter. Just kill her."

"Req, let me play," Mako whined as he wiggled his fingers toward me.

"No. I have things to do and I want these two dealt with. I gave my word, so kill her and I can finish this one off."

Well, that wasn't exactly subtle. Belladonna let out a low moan. "Lark. Please don't die."

"Kill her now!" Requiem roared.

Snarling, Mako lunged at me. This was it. I sidestepped and grabbed his throat with both hands. Or tried to anyway. I only managed to catch him with my left hand; he punched my right forearm knocking it away. Squeezing my fingers tightly around his neck, I dug my nails into the flesh, gripping with everything I had. Years of working the fields in the Rim made my hands strong, the muscles in my forearms like iron bands. He squirmed like a fish on a hook, eyes bugging. The crowd above us roared, their energy and excitement contagious and buoying me.

Mako twisted and kicked out at me, clawed toes digging furrows into my thighs and hips. Blood tinted the water, but I didn't take my eyes from him, couldn't let him go. This was my chance. He'd underestimated me and now I had him dead to rights. But if I let go I knew I wouldn't get another chance.

His fingers scrabbled at my hand as he tried to pry my fingers off. A shot of adrenaline-fueled fear lanced me as I stared at him. His skin glowed with a soft blue that swirled up his arms.

He was calling on his connection to the water and from the intent I saw in the power, he was going to drown me. Or at least, he was going to try. I got my right hand up and wrapped it around his throat, as the water yanked my feet out from under me. We went down and I kept my eyes open, salt stinging them. I couldn't let go.

Mako fought to get closer to me, his shorter, muscle-bound arms reaching for my eyes as I stared him down through the swirling pink water. His face darkened to a deep purple as I bore down with both hands, crushing his windpipe. His gills fluttered against the tops of my hands . . . gills.

He was breathing the water, it wouldn't matter if I crushed his trachea completely, he could breathe underwater. I had to destroy his gills. Mother goddess help me.

I shifted my hands up his neck and slid my fingers into the

fluttering flaps of fleshy material. Cool water rushed over my skin, the movement of tiny bits that felt like layered leaves, as I stared into Mako's eyes. A flash of fear danced over his face as I drove my fingers in deep. I tried not to think about the burning in my lungs, the pain of holding my breath as I fought with everything I had.

Mako grabbed at me, raking his fingers down my arms, his reach just an inch short of being able to hook into my face. So instead, he grabbed my vest and yanked the buckles, baring my chest to him. No, that was not going to happen. I tucked my feet up between us and kicked at his hands, barely keeping him from grabbing my breasts and tearing them from my chest.

I had to end this fast.

Hooking my fingers deep into the gills on the right side of his neck, I felt for the connective tissue. I didn't think about what I was doing, didn't think about anything but stopping him as his fingers brushed my sensitive skin, clawing at me. Curling my fingers around the tissue, I pulled, yanking the gills on that side of his neck apart. His mouth opened and blood pooled out around us. I lost sight of him completely, but I didn't let go.

I worked my left hand into the gills on that side of his neck. His foot caught me in my gut, and he pushed off. But he was too late. I had my fingers into the edges of his gills and as he pushed, he ripped his own neck apart. I kicked away from him, fighting to get to the surface.

The water stilled and I shot up and out of it to suck in a lungful of air. In my hand was not only his gills, but a huge section of his trachea that came with it. Gulping a lungful of air and treading water I waited to see if another attack would come, but nothing did. The water lowered once more until I could stand. Only then did I start to take stock of my own body: open gashes along my thighs, the punctures in my stomach, and a spinning in my head from holding my breath too long.

The water around me was dark with blood. Did I move and hope

I could at least put my back to the wall, or did I hold still and pray Mako couldn't see where I was any more than I could see him?

An air bubble popped up across from me and I tensed. Mako's back floated to the surface and bobbed, face down. A ruse?

Above us, the crowd I'd forgotten about cheered. The water drained completely and the footing I stood on began to rise. Mako stayed face down, chunks of meat and gills floating around the sides of his neck, his trachea in my hand. I threw it to the ground and refastened my vest.

The slow clapping of one person turned me around. Requiem smiled at me, his teeth bright white and far too big for his face. The smile was cold. "Well done. I must say I am surprised. Where did you learn to fight? Enders always play by the rules but that . . . that was truly impressive."

"I did play by the rules, though he didn't. He raised the water. I suppose that means you owe us." I knew no such thing, but I was pissed. Not to mention the fact he'd said he was looking for a way to kill us both.

Dolph, headed my way with a blanket, stopped in his tracks. His mouth moved over three words. *Don't do it.*

I glared at Requiem. But it was Belladonna who spoke. "Your champion cheated. We all saw it." Her color was slowly coming back. Ayu was at her side and obviously had been helping her. "What will you give us in compensation, Requiem?"

Requiem looked from Belladonna to me, then back to her. His button black eyes were thoughtful, a calculating mind behind them. That much was obvious. "Well played, Ambassador. Well played. We will have a dinner in your honor tomorrow night, and you shall be our guests of the highest standing. There, I shall give you your . . . gifts."

I gathered my weapons, doing my best to attach them as we walked from the coliseum. Dolph helped me out of the arena, and Ayu helped Belladonna. Around us, the other Undines parted. Without fail, each Undine we passed gave me a quick bow, a few reaching out to touch me. A mark of honor; I had done what none of their Enders had been capable of. I should have felt proud, but I wasn't. We were in so much hot water I couldn't see the way out, and the death of one violent bastard wasn't about to save us.

No one spoke as Dolph and Ayu took us to a sumptuous room decked out in pearls, silk sheets, and carpet made of a material I couldn't identify. Some sort of sea moss was my guess by the way it gave under my feet. All I knew was it was soft enough to lie on and sleep for days.

Ayu helped Belladonna into bed and then gave me a vial. "Drink it, your wounds will heal faster and you will be ready."

I held the vial to my lips. "Ready for what?"

She looked to Dolph behind me, and just shook her head. They left me standing, staring at the large double doors as they shut behind them. The not so subtle click of the door being locked chilled my spine. I downed the vial of potion, the salty and sweet taste refreshing me even as my body slumped with fatigue. I should have stayed awake, should have forced myself to guard her. The exhaustion though was too strong for me.

I flopped onto the bed next to Bella. "I guess we'll find out tomorrow what we need to be ready for."

She opened one gray eye and looked me over. "Let's hope we can go one day here without getting injured. Shall we try that?"

I dropped a hand over hers, surprised to feel her fingers tighten around mine. "Sure, I'm game to try anything once."

Closing my eyes, I let sleep tumble me down. And prayed to the mother goddess we would both make it out of the Deep alive.

Chapter 7

We slept through much of the next day, our bodies drugged with whatever Ayu had given us both to help speed our healing. When I woke, Belladonna was already up and searching through the closet. Actually, it had been her exasperated grunt and the thump of something large hitting the ground that snapped me out of my deep sleep.

"Lark, the clothes they have here, they are ridiculous. Look at this." She tossed something toward the bed. It was a dress made of fish net. I picked it up by one edge. "Maybe it's supposed to go over something else. Like layers."

"That sea worm wants us to dress like common prostitutes." Her outrage was all the more amusing because of our previous conversation. Maybe she'd decided she wasn't going to tease the men to get her information now. Then again, maybe even Belladonna had standards when it came to those she was willing to taunt. Requiem was not one she wanted to get any closer to than she had to. I certainly didn't.

From the bed, I watched her move, amazed that she barely limped. The bite marks in her leg were mostly healed with only tiny pink lines marking where they had been.

I slid from the bed with a groan. My thighs burned and I rubbed a hand over each. The furrows from Mako's claw-tipped toes were ridged, sore, and itched like fire ants had been nipping at me all night.

"Lark," Bella's voice was soft as she stood in front of me. "No one has ever fought for me." She looked away, her throat bobbing as she swallowed hard. "I thought you were going to leave me there to die, but you didn't."

I shrugged. "Family is family. I promised I wouldn't let you die. Maybe it's been too long since we've spent time together, but you should know I always keep my promises."

She gave me a weak grin and swiftly changed the subject. "We both have to dress for the dinner." She held up two pieces of fish net, one in each hand. "Do you want to wear the fish net or the fish net?"

I stood and shook my head. "I'm your bodyguard. I'm not going anywhere without my—" I reached for my spear and found nothing. A quick check of my body, all my weapons were gone except the tiny knife tucked into my vest. The knife Ash had given me for just this reason. Our only weapon that stood between us and Requiem was a wee tiny knife.

Not exactly the protection I was hoping for.

Belladonna lifted a sheer piece of silk, light green and shimmering. I put a hand on hers.

"Bella, we have to play this right or no matter what Requiem said, we're going to have our heads handed to us on a platter."

"I know."

"He thinks you caused the earthquake on the island."

Her eyes widened. "Why would he think that?"

I took the sheer green material and folded it in half, then motioned for her to turn away from me. I spoke as I wrapped her body in the silk. "It makes sense. Father doesn't know what I am capable of, no one does. So to Requiem it looks as though Father has sent an ambassador who can cause tsunamis. An ambassador to be feared."

She glanced over her shoulder as I tied off the silk. I'd wrapped her from just above her chest to just above her knee. Scrounging in the closet I found a second cut of sheer material, a pale blue dotted with seed pearls.

"Lark, that means he's afraid of me," she breathed. "It gives us power."

I wasn't so sure. "Maybe. But he's wary of me because I killed Mako."

A slow smile slid across her face and for a moment she looked so like her mother that I stopped moving. "We have more power than you realize, Lark."

"I don't give two worm shits about power. We just need to survive as long as it takes to get us the hell out of here. I think we can both agree that if Father is to back anyone, it should be Requiem's sister, Finley."

I took the seed pearl material, tied a swath of it over her breasts which finally gave her decent coverage, then wrapped it in a slow loop down her body, tying it off at the bottom.

"You missed your calling, Lark. You could have been a fabulous dressmaker."

I snorted. "I'll keep it in mind if this job doesn't pan out."

She giggled and then stopped. "You look terrible. We need to clean you up too."

There was no denying she was right. I was covered in blood, bits of Mako's gills hung from my hair and my leather was crusted with dried salt.

"No. Let them see me like this. Covered in their champion's blood. Requiem . . . I don't think he's afraid of us, Bella. Not for an instant. He is not a stupid man."

"He should be afraid of us," she said, her haughty tone telling me her arrogance was back full force. Which in that instance was a very good thing, seeing as we needed to face him down at dinner.

I helped arrange her hair so it hung in long loose curls around her face. The length spooling down her back helped to give a bit more skin coverage. The only jewelry we had left between us was Griffin's gift to me. The tooth corded on leather that kept me safe from the lung burrowers. The tooth of a griffin was a powerful talisman.

I slipped it off my neck and over hers. "Here, put this on. A reminder to them that while you may wear their pearls, you are a child of the earth. A child of the beasts and a power to be reckoned with."

Her back straightened and she covered my hand with hers. "Thank you."

A knock came at the door and we turned. I stepped back, allowing Belladonna to take the lead.

"Enter," she called out, sounding every inch the princess she was. Barefoot and wearing material meant to demean her, she swayed forward as the door opened. A tall gangly boy who couldn't have been out of his teen years, and looked to be a younger version of Dolph, goggled at her.

"Spit it out, boy." She snapped her fingers and I fought not to smile. Maybe Father was right to have sent her after all. Then I remembered he might be trying to bump us both off. I had no way of telling Ash how poor things were going.

"The dinner is ready." He gave her a bow, which also gave him a chance to check out her bare legs. I reached out and put a hand on Bella's shoulder.

"We need to send a message to your father."

She frowned at me. "Boy, how do we do that?"

He swallowed hard. "You could send a seabird. Would you like me to get you one?"

"Yes, immediately." Belladonna snapped her fingers at him a second time.

He backed out, closing the doors behind him.

"That was good thinking, Lark."

The boy, Urchin by his stuttering introduction the second time around, didn't take long. He thrust a piece of paper at us, a seagull tucked under his wing. "He'll take the message right to the Rim."

Belladonna took a piece of paper and I all but snatched it from her. "I need something to write with." She frowned at me, but blessedly didn't argue.

We searched the room; there wasn't a single pencil or quill. I should get into the habit of always carrying a bag with the bare necessities. Parchment, a quill, small things that could be useful even if my weapons were taken away.

"Here," Belladonna handed me a hunk of kohl we'd used around her eyes that was smooth on one end. "This should work."

I took it and smoothed the paper against the wall. There had to be a way to say things were going wrong. That we were in trouble. The message would go through Ash first; at least, that was what I was counting on. If Father truly was against us, he would ignore the message, but Ash said he would come for us. And I was banking on that. No matter how badly I wanted to prove myself capable of taking care of Belladonna and this assignment, we were in over our heads.

Our boat is sideways and taking on water.

The words were thick and dark, the lines scratched in with more than a little aggression. I folded the paper and slipped it into the carrier on the seagull's leg. The gull gave a squawk as I took it from Urchin and strode to our balcony. Flinging the windows open, I tossed the gull high into the air. It flapped its wings, settled into the air currents and flew to the west. At least it was going the right way.

Belladonna raised one eyebrow at me. I stared at her, keeping my face carefully blank. "Princess, I do believe they are waiting for you."

A tip of her head at me, she clapped her hands together sharply. "Boy, we're ready."

The doors creaked open and the boy stuck his head in, color

rising in his cheeks. "I said my name is Urchin, and I am an Ender in training."

"Fine, fine." Belladonna waved a hand at him. "Take us to dinner, I'm starving."

Another awkward bow from Urchin as a glower shimmered over his face, and then he led the way through the long halls. They stretched in seemingly endless lengths, the ceilings so far above our heads I could barely make them out.

The palace was built with soft pastels, pinks, blues, creamy whites, and yellows. Like a dream, gauzy and surreal. I drew in a deep breath through my mouth, tasting salt and the night air cool against my tongue. Tiny orbs of water filled with weird fish that glowed were strung along the pathways, seemingly flickering in the ocean breeze. Their light dimmed suddenly with a particular hard snap of wind; an impossibility, yet there it was. Shadows and light danced across our path and the fish globes struggled to stay lit, and I knew the moment for what it was.

An omen of things to come.

Urchin cleared his throat, his long fingers tapping against his thighs. He stopped at a large doorway, stepping in front of us. "My father wanted me to give you this. But asked that you burn it after you read it."

Belladonna took the note, read it, and handed it to me. "Does it mean anything to you?"

I skimmed the note, frowning as I read.

Let nothing pass the gates to your home, for you will not see the dawn if you do.

Lifting the note, I held it to one of the candles. The paper caught quickly and burned down to my fingers. I flipped the remaining ashes to the ground. "No, but that doesn't mean we won't understand it when the time comes." At least that was what I was hoping.

Urchin nodded, pushed the doors open. Made of sandstone and engraved with scenes of battle, I only caught a glimpse of the images—tentacles reaching from the depths of the ocean—before my eyes were drawn forward.

Though the room was fairly well decorated, my eyes could only see one thing—a single table a hundred feet long stretched the length of the room and laden with food and drink. The smell was overwhelming, and my stomach growled, urging me forward.

Belladonna put her hands to her stomach. "Do not let me make a pig of myself, Lark. I fear I will if allowed free rein."

I fought the grin that wanted to spread across my face. "I might let you, just so I can say that I saw you stuff your face."

Her shoulders shook with repressed laughter, something I wasn't sure I'd ever seen. I knew why, though. We were giddy with hunger and thirst, our bodies making us fools.

Urchin led us through the room and I struggled not to stare at the lay out. Above our heads hung a massive kelp bed held aloft by something I couldn't see, lit with tiny lights and strung with pearls and starfish. I froze as something moved within the swirling plant's beds. A sea otter swam through the kelp as if it were water over our heads and not air. That display would take a lot of power, but I didn't see any Sylph's—air elementals—around holding it together.

The tiny creature grabbed at a fish that shot past and swirled in a circle as it played. A second otter joined, and they twinned around one another in a dance that should have been impossible.

"They don't know they aren't in water. The Sylph ambassador set it up before she . . . left."

I turned to see Ayu staring at the otter with me. "*Left*. Is that what we're calling it now?"

"For now, yes. You'd best hurry. Your ambassador is ahead of you, and I doubt you want to let her out of arm's length."

She was right, Belladonna was sitting at her assigned chair. Her hands trembled as she reached for the goblet at her place setting.

Lifted it to her mouth.

Tipped her head as her lips parted. The gates to the home of her body opened.

A cold shot of fear lanced my heart.

"Belladonna! Manners!" I yelled across the room at her, making everyone stop and stare at us. I strode forward. "You know better. Are you the ambassador or am I?"

Her eyes widened and then narrowed. "Ender, you overstep." She lifted the goblet again as I reached her.

I slapped it out of her hands.

"Your father would be embarrassed."

She shot to her feet.

Requiem stood behind her. "Ladies, please. There is no need to be so formal. Of course, let your ambassador dig into the meal. It was especially prepared with her in mind."

"Of course, it was." I reached out and grabbed Bella's wrist, gripping it until the bones under my hands ground together. She whimpered, but I didn't look at her, I kept my eyes on Requiem. "Perhaps you would like to share a goblet with my ambassador, in a show of good faith?"

Belladonna looked at me and I glanced at her, softening my hold on her wrist. I saw the understanding hit her and she relaxed. "I think that is a wonderful idea." I let go, knowing she understood as well as I did.

Let nothing pass the gates to your home, for you will not see the dawn. The food and drink were poisoned. We were no more safe now than we had been when we first stepped foot into the Deep.

Requiem shook his head and patted his belly. "Alas, I have already eaten my fill, but here, I will drink to your . . . health." He scooped up the goblet and downed it in a single gulp.

How, how could he do that if it was poisoned? I was sure I was right though and was staking our lives on it.

"So much for manners," Belladonna muttered under her breath. Louder, she said. "Shall we sit and converse then?" She didn't touch the food, and relief swept through me.

Requiem gave her a nod and they sat side-by-side launching into a discussion about the best ways to rule. By force, bribery, fear, or adoration. I stepped back to give them room. Not because they needed it, really. More because it was what was expected of me.

The night dragged, the smell of food made my mouth fill with saliva and my mind wander. Undines began to leave in twos and threes before Requiem stood. "Lovely speaking with you, Belladonna. You are a creature of fascinating contradictions. Ambassador, princess, lady of culture, and yet there is so much power in you."

She tipped her head slightly. "A woman no matter how plain she seems is always a sea of mystery, Requiem. Surely at your advanced age you must know that by now?"

Oh snap. I had to bite the inside of my mouth to keep from laughing out loud.

Requiem's eyes darkened. "You play a dangerous game."

I stepped forward. "And you aren't?"

He raised his eyes to mine and I realized we were pretty much alone, the three of us at the head of the table. "You two are free to roam wherever you like for the remainder of your stay. Just be warned that not all of my people welcome you as I do, so I cannot guarantee your safety outside your rooms."

I didn't stop the snort that escaped me. Requiem ignored me and dropped his eyes to Belladonna. "Your mother, is she well?"

Belladonna stiffened, her whole body suddenly vibrating with tension. "She's quite well, thank you."

A slow smile spread across his lips. "I do believe it has been years since I spoke with her. Perhaps I should send her a message, invite her to see me crowned." He rubbed his hand over his jaw.

Belladonna stood, pushing her chair back. "I am tired. It has been a long two days. Goodnight, Requiem."

She took a measured pace, not hurrying but not dawdling either. I walked at her side, glancing back to Requiem. His smile only widened as our eyes met. He lifted a hand and waved.

The walk to our room was silent. Belladonna went straight in and began to pace. I stood in the doorway. "Stay here, I'm going to see about some food."

"Everything will be poisoned, Lark." Her gray eyes were clouded with frustration and more than a little fear.

"How can that be? They all ate. Even Requiem downed a goblet."

She rolled her eyes at me. "I forget you didn't take the schooling we did. Every family has things they are resistant to. Things they can ingest or be infected with, with no affect."

I gripped the edge of the door. "And the Undines?"

"Puffer fish."

Hands on my hips, I knew our options were not good. As much as we were a long-lived people and could handle a lot of injuries, and even go a for a good length of time without food, we couldn't go forever without eating and drinking. "I'm going to go see what I can find. You get a fire going so we can cook if I manage to find a fish or two." I pointed at the blackened and cracked fireplace that probably hadn't seen a flame in years. She nodded, not arguing.

"Bella . . ."

"Why do you keep calling me that?" she whispered. "No one calls me that anymore."

I shrugged. "Because right now, you are the sister I remember. Not the one Cassava created, and I am hoping you see that. Lock the door behind me." Backing up, I waited until she shut the door in my face and I heard the lock slide into place. I put a hand on the door, wondering just how changed my sister was. Or was it all a ruse to suck me under the belief I could trust her?

I dropped my hand and backed away. Only time would tell.

Not something either of us had.

Chapter 8

Passing Undines here and there, I kept my pace brisk. As if I knew where I was going and was allowed to do whatever I was doing. No one stopped me; they hardly even looked up as I walked through the palace.

There were more important things than food. Like answers to my questions, and there was only one place I could think to start.

I found the healers' room with relative ease and let myself in. "I'll be with you in a moment," a voice called out.

I didn't answer, just wandered deeper into the room. Looking at the things laid out. Tools of the trade. Scalpels, pincers, vials, and potions, a mortar and pestle with something shiny and red half ground in it. The shiny red bits moved, and I jumped back, bumping into one of the tables.

"Ender, I'm surprised to see you here." Ayu spoke softly to

my left. I put a hand on the table, the material under my fingers soft and warm.

As if a body had only recently lain on it.

I snatched my hand up. "I want to speak with Finley. I want to see if there is something we can do to support her."

She let out a tired sigh and shook her head. "No one has seen the princess in months. She is locked up in her rooms with only guards to keep her company."

"And if she's not dead before the crowning ceremony?"

Her eyes met mine, the sorrow in them deep. "I don't believe that is even an option for Requiem. You can do nothing to help her, Ender. Though, I see it in you. You have a healer's heart and you want to help. It is admirable, but a deadly desire in the Deep."

She may have been right, but I had to see for myself. "Would she make a better ruler?"

"Anyone would make a better ruler. Even Blue, Requiem's bitch of a wife, would make a better ruler, for she does not have her husband's cruelty or intelligence. If she were not missing, perhaps she could help temper Requiem. But she was 'misplaced' soon after the king died." Ayu shook her head, braids dancing. "No, there is nothing to be done for it. Requiem has a stranglehold on our people, one we cannot break free of."

I snorted. "You all have given up so easily. I thought the Undines were some legendary family with strength to the core of them."

Expecting her to be angry, and lash out me, I was shocked when she didn't. "Not when it has been beaten out of them, Ender."

I backed slowly out of the room. "Then perhaps you deserve Requiem as a leader, since you are not willing to stand up to him." Her eyes followed me and when I turned at the door I heard her whisper.

"Perhaps this is our punishment for our pride, Ender. Remember that. There is always a downfall when pride lifts you too high."

Shutting the door behind me, I leaned against it, thinking. So the people here were downtrodden, and though I felt bad for them, I also didn't want to get pulled into their struggles.

Who was I kidding? We were yanked, kicking and screaming, into this. Now it was a question of who would survive this growing storm as it gathered on the horizon.

The Undines, or me and Bella.

An older Undine, his hair white and hanging in long curls to his waist, approached from the far end of the hallway. He leaned on a cane, limping as he walked, and his ears stuck out from the sides of his head like handles on a jug. But his eyes were kind, and they didn't shy from me as he drew close. "Terraling, you look lost. Can I help you?"

Terraling. That was what my family—the earth elementals—was known as outside the Rim, and for a moment the name caught me off guard it had been so long since I'd heard it.

Putting my right hand over my heart I gave him a bow from the waist. "Thank you. Can you direct me to the kitchens?"

"I'm going that way myself, perhaps you will escort me?" He raised his brows, the thick bushy things touching his hairline.

I bowed again and allowed him to lead, a half step ahead of me.

"How do you like the Deep so far, Ender?"

Struggling to find the right words, I cleared my throat before answering. "It is not what I expected."

"Ah, things outside our own families rarely are."

"I'm sorry, but I didn't catch your name." Perhaps he was someone important. Or worse, sided with Requiem.

"I didn't give it. Around here, it is best no one knows when help is given. That is a sure way to spend the remainder of your life stuffed into the cells."

I licked my lips, knowing I was taking a chance. "Like the other ambassadors?"

The old man didn't look at me, but I saw the tension run across his shoulders and his eyes watered suddenly, as if he were on the verge of tears.

Looked like I'd hit my mark, but even so, he said nothing of my question.

"Well, here we are. The kitchens. If I can make a suggestion as to the fare you are about to partake?" He turned to face me, eyes serious.

"Of course."

"I find the fruit to be the best form of sustenance these days. Only the fruit. And perhaps a little rainwater from the outer levels." He gave me a wink and I bowed to him a second time.

"I will accede to your wisdom. Thank you."

He said nothing more, only turned and continued down the hall to wherever it was he was going.

I watched him until he was out of sight, around the corner, the steady thump of his cane fading. Putting a hand to the doors, I tugged. They were locked, though I wasn't terribly surprised. If you're going to poison the food, you aren't going to just leave it out for anyone to get into.

I pulled my dagger from my vest and worked it between the door and the wall. Jiggling and turning, I was rewarded with a soft click of the door opening. Looking at the blade, I was surprised it hadn't cracked with the force I'd exerted. If I made it back to the Rim . . . no, *when* I made it back to the Rim, I hoped Ash would hold to his word and teach me the art of blacksmithing.

I slipped through the door and into the room, dim shadows obscuring everything. Everything except the muffled whispers and the subtle movement of bodies crouching low to the ground.

I tightened my grip on my dagger and stepped into the room. Children's voices, high and uncertain, whispered to each other and pulled me forward.

"Who is it?"

"I don't know. She's not an Undine."

I cleared my throat. "I'm an Ender from the Rim. Who are you?"

A tiny head popped up from behind a kitchen table. A young Undine, maybe ten years old, his eyes sunken into his head and cheeks hollow with hunger. "We just came to get something to eat."

I put my dagger away, tucking it under my vest. Not easy to grab, but I didn't want to lose it. The two children watched me and I was reminded kids were often far more honest than any adult.

So while the old man had given good advice, a second opinion wouldn't hurt. "Me too. Perhaps you can help me. Is there anything in here that hasn't been tainted with puffer fish?"

The little boy searched around and finally handed me a large mango. "Here, the fruit is clean. Everything else has puffer in it by the smell." He gave a loud sniff to emphasize his point. I was glad the old man had been telling the truth, at least.

I took the proffered fruit, peeled the skin with my teeth then bit into it as I watched the two kids, twins by the looks of them, scurry around the kitchen. "What are your names?"

"No, we can't tell you that." The boy shook his head. "You could tell . . . Requiem"—he stumbled over the name—"we were here and he would send his sharks to eat us."

His sister nodded. "They'd skin us alive."

How a shark could skin them alive, I didn't know, but a child's fears were always based on true possibility.

It seemed as though everyone within the Deep was afraid to be known.

Another direction then. "Why do you take the food from here? Why not just go fishing?"

They stopped and the boy looked up at me. "Requiem made it so all the fish will only come to him. Mama said it's so we will make him king because he will feed us then. Mama hates him."

I rocked back on my heels, eating my mango, wondering how far I could push the questions. "Do you two know where the princess's rooms are?"

The little boy didn't stop stuffing his bag as he answered. "No one does. She's hidden away."

Now that was interesting. How was it that no one could know where the crown princess was? Or maybe they just didn't know because they were kids.

I gathered more fruit, mostly mangoes and bananas, when a

thought struck me. "How did you two get in here anyway? The door was locked."

Grinning, the little boy pointed at the grate under his feet. "Pipes run all under the Deep. Since you're an Terraling, you just got to be able to hold your breath." He stepped off the grate, slid his fingers through it and flicked it open. He and his sister—with their bags of food—slid into the water, pulling the grate closed over them with barely a splash.

With the children gone, I slipped out of the kitchen and made my way to our room. The matter of the food being withheld from the people explained a lot. The lack of motivation, the sheer fact so few people were up and around and those who were barely registered anyone around them. The only ones eating well were those at the banquet. The nobles and high-ranking officials.

There was a light under the door of our room when I reached it. I knocked softly. "Bella."

The sound of feet and voices . . . I jiggled the handle, a thread of fear slicing through me. "Bella."

Feet on the padded floor, the rustle of cloth and then the door opened, but it was not who I expected to be standing there.

Familiar honey-gold eyes stared into mine, blond hair catching the light. His leather vest was open at the throat, baring an expanse of sun-darkened skin. "Ender, your timing as always is impeccable."

I swallowed hard, unable to speak, my mind caught up with what had been going on behind the closed door before I'd knocked. "I found mangoes." The urge to slap my head with my hand was strong, but I held the bag in front of me and pushed my way in. "You got my message then . . ."

Belladonna was stretched out on the bed on her side, her hand resting in the curve of her waist. A smile on her lips like the cat that had snuck into the creamery and had its fill.

I laid the bag of fruit on the table, reminding myself that Ash didn't like Belladonna in the least.

He folded his arms over his chest. "No, I didn't get your message.

Your father decided it would be best if we were both out of the way while the ambassador from the Pit decides our fate. You weren't the only one killing Enders." Ah, there was that.

I narrowed my eyes at him, looking him over. He didn't get the message, which meant he didn't understand how much trouble we were in.

Which could mean he wasn't here to help us at all. I didn't want to believe it of him, but if our father was trying to bump us off, and wanted to be sure it happened . . . sending another Ender would be good insurance.

"How did you get in here? Belladonna, I told you not to let anyone in except me."

Belladonna sat up and I put myself between her and Ash. His eyes widened slightly as he took in my stance. "You don't think I'm here to hurt you, do you?"

"How did you get in here?" I repeated. My muscles strummed with building adrenaline. I didn't want to fight him, but what option would I have if he attacked my sister?

He folded his arms and stared hard at me. "The humans send in boats full of food. How do you think the fruit gets here? I hitched a ride with one of them. As to this room. I knocked, the princess let me in."

Belladonna laughed softly. "How brilliant. Perhaps we should try that next time, Lark, instead of rowing into shark infested waters."

Heat suffused my cheeks. It was a smart move, but how was I to know about the shipping lanes? No one had suggested it to me. There were a lot of things not adding up.

"Ash, I need to speak to the ambassador privately." I pointed to the door.

His eyebrows shot up, but he backed out closing the door behind him.

I turned to see Belladonna on her knees on the bed. I put a finger to my lips as I approached her. Crouching beside the bed I forced myself to think like a chess player. Where would I put the pieces if I wanted to take out those who caused me grief?

Belladonna put a hand on my shoulder, her gray eyes thoughtful. "I think he's here to make sure we don't survive." Her words echoed my own suspicions.

Pain zinged through me at the thought of not being able to trust Ash, but I nodded. "I agree. There was no talk of sending him away, why Father would send both of his Enders at the same time . . . this doesn't make sense."

"What do we do? Requiem is the devil incarnate. Do you know he is starving his people?"

"How did you figure that out?"

She snorted softly. "At the banquet. The things said and unsaid were all there if you know what you're looking for. How did you find out?"

"Kids in the kitchen. Requiem is keeping the fish at bay somehow so the people will let him be king if only to be fed."

The silence between us lasted only a minute or two, but in it I knew we were allies finally. I put my hand over hers on my shoulder.

"We play their game better than them. That is our only chance."

She chewed her bottom lip. "And Ash?"

"He needs to stay in the dark. If he's here at Father's request, to make sure we don't survive, he can't know we are working together."

Bella's eyes darted to the door, then me. "You're stronger than him, aren't you?"

I knew what the real question was. Could I kill him? Shaking my head, I didn't answer her. She grabbed my face. "You have to be. Or we're both dead."

Chapter 9

To say the night passed in companionable silence would be a lie. Belladonna slept on the bed, and I lay beside her wide awake and staring at the ceiling. Listening to Ash's slow even breathing as he sat against the doors. Guarding them. I pulled out the thin knife he'd given me, tucking it under my pillow. Just in case he decided to come at me, at least I wouldn't be fumbling with my vest.

My mind whirled with questions and possibilities, the darkness of the night seeming to urge my thoughts into the worst possible scenarios. Why had Ash really come? Was he telling the truth? Something about what he'd said didn't sit right with me and that was the core of my unease. He wasn't honest. I felt it with every breath I took.

Ash lied, and that truth ate at me.

Beside me, Belladonna rolled over, her face peaceful in sleep. The morning sun spilled in around us, backlighting her and making her hair glow. Here was the sister I remembered. Not the sister she had become. I touched her forehead, smoothing back her hair, wondering if the damage Cassava had done could be undone. Like the mother goddess had done for me.

"No, I don't want to," she whimpered, her face crinkling up and tears pooling in the corners of her eyes. She jerked away from me, her eyes opening, but she didn't see me. I knew that look. I'd seen it in the mirror more than once. Belladonna saw her past and she didn't like what she looked at, saw all that she couldn't escape, no matter how far she ran.

I spit out the first thing that came to my mind. "You want the shower first?"

Scrubbing her hands through her hair she nodded. "Yes. Come help me out of this dress." There was really no need to help her, but we still had to discuss our plan and see if we could find a way to survive the Deep.

My eyes were dry and crusted over with dirt, salt, and flecks of gore still. I stood and stretched my arms over my head, limbs protesting the long night unmoving. I glanced at Ash.

He still slept. His head leaned against the door, eyes closed.

I headed to the bathroom attached to our room.

Belladonna was already naked and scrubbing herself under the flow of water.

Half the room was set up as a shower, the walls tiled in pale blue marble flecked with black streaks, but the base of the shower was a pure white sand. I slid a hand over the marble to the dangling handle next to the shower. Guessing, I pulled on it.

Water poured out like a miniature waterfall. I stepped under the flow, gasping at the temperature. Not hot by any means, the water was clean, fresh, and smelling of rain. It beckoned. I couldn't help opening my mouth and gulping down a few gallons, finally quenching my thirst. I scooped up handfuls of sand from the bottom of the shower and scrubbed it over my skin and hair while the water pounded around me.

Finally feeling refreshed, I stepped out of the shower, but let it run. I grabbed a towel for myself and handed one to my sister. She wrapped it around her body and we tucked our heads close together, the rushing water drowning out our words.

"I'm going to find Ambassador Barkley, or whatever is left of him. You make friends with Requiem. Take Ash."

She nodded. "Be careful, Lark. We only have each other."

I flicked the pull handle of the showers, shutting the water off and turned. Ash stood there, watching.

"Ambassador. Your presence is requested." He stepped to the side. Behind him was a human slave. The first we'd seen.

Belladonna sucked in a sharp breath and I struggled not to do the same. Skeletally thin, I wasn't even sure if I looked at a man or a woman, an adult or a child. Draped in a thin white cloth, the material only accentuated the jutting bones and jagged hollows where flesh should have been.

The slave held out a silver platter, arms shaking with the effort. He spoke, carefully. "Requiem would like to eat you. Eat *with* you, I mean." I darted forward and grabbed the platter. On it was a single note with Bella's name written across it in bold script. I handed it to her. She cracked it open.

"Requested to dine with him. Again." She threw the letter down, strode into the other room, and grabbed two pieces of fruit. "Here, eat this. Your body offends me."

She shoved the fruit at the slave who stared up at her, then fell to his knees as he jammed the fruit into his mouth. Crying, he ate, and I couldn't look at him. This was the ugly truth of the Undines. Even without Requiem at the head, they thought nothing of having slaves. Even that old man I'd met the night before, he'd seemed kind. And yet, he likely had his own set of slaves to tend to him.

I dropped my towel and went to grab my clothes. Which were no longer on the floor where I'd left them. Scooping my towel back up I wrapped it around my body, tying it off along my chest. The flash of white cloth slipping through the door caught my eye.

The human slaves were quick with their chores it seemed.

"They'll bring them back," Ash said. "The slaves are very good at what they do."

My jaw dropped and Belladonna elbowed me hard. "Of course they are. See, Lark, they even brought us clothes to wear."

On the bed were two outfits. Or what passed in the Deep as outfits. A swath of black silk lay stretched across the bed next to a pure white swath of silk. White was what the slaves wore.

I picked up the white silk, knowing what it meant to put it on, to admit I had no value. Requiem knew I was a bastard. "Want to guess which one of us this is for?"

Belladonna sucked in a sharp breath. "He wouldn't go so far."

I shrugged. "We don't really know him other than the fact he tried to kill us at least twice and me three times." I hated to admit I didn't understand the games and politics, but Belladonna knew this world better than I did. My jaw tightened, but I managed to speak. "Do you think I should wear it?"

She fingered it. "No, I think I will wear it. It's a better color on me, black is too harsh."

Ash grunted softly. "What are you up to, Belladonna?"

She batted her eyes at him. "Whatever do you mean, Ender? I wish only for Requiem to see I serve him while I am here. Do you not think the white is fitting?"

Clever, clever girl. Lips twitching, I fought back the smile as I helped her wind her body into the white silk. She was right; the white did look fantastic against her dark hair and smoky eyes. Her hand went to the griffin tooth still around her neck. "This is too crass with this silk. You wear it, Lark." She all but flicked the necklace across to me. I caught it and slid it over my head. Why had she given it back? Perhaps she really didn't like it, maybe she really did think it clashed with the white silk.

Of course, she didn't know that it was magical either.

Dressed as much as she was going to be, Belladonna held out a hand to Ash. "Come, take me. Let us explore this place."

Ash hesitated, glanced at me still in my towel then took her hand. "Of course."

So well trained as an Ender, he didn't think of breaking the rules. Of turning down a command from someone superior to him.

The door closed behind them and I dropped the towel forgetting the slave who'd brought us the message. He cleared his throat. "Lady, do you need help with the silk?" I nodded.

"Yes, please. I didn't think to ask for help before they left."

He moved to my side and I wondered how long he had before he would be dead. Even with the influx of calories he'd just had, I knew he didn't have the strength to last more than a few days. Yet, his hands were still deft as they wove the black silk around my body, pulling it tight and tying it off at my waist. "There you go. Right as rain."

"What is your name?"

He smiled, his eyes going distant. "Don't know if I remember anymore. It's been so long."

I licked my lips. "Has it always been this bad, for the slaves?"

"No, lady, it hasn't. It will get worse, though." His brown eyes flicked over me. "You should leave. While you can."

With a wobbly bow, he began to back out of the room.

"Wait. The cells, where are they? How do I get to them?"

The slave paused and then pointed down to the floor.

"Please," I begged. "I'm trying to make things better." A half truth, but I would say anything to make him trust me.

He closed his eyes, trembling where he stood. "The slave quarters. They reside above them. But I've heard there is a secret entrance, on the same level as the kitchen. That is all I can tell you."

I reached under the pillow and pulled my one dagger out. Ash still had all his weapons, not one was removed from him. Yet another strike against him, as much as it hurt to admit.

Digging around the closet, I came up with a studded belt. Too big for my waist, I slid it over my hips at an angle. From it, I hung the dagger's sheath. Stepping out of the room I headed left. Ayu would be of no help, and other than Dolph, I didn't know anyone else. The cells would be on the lowest levels. That made sense, but the secret entrance . . . That might be my best bet.

Searching the hallways was a strange thing because there was no one around. No one except the same old man I'd met the night before. We passed each other several times with nothing more than a nod here and there.

Once I caught him asleep on a bench that rested across from the kitchens. There was no one to stop me as I slid my fingers along the edges of the walls looking for a cut in the rough material. Hours passed and the heat rose. Sweating freely, the black silk stuck to my skin, clinging tightly to my body.

"Ender Lark?"

I turned slowly to see Urchin, Dolph's boy, behind me. How much could I trust him?

"Urchin? That's your name, isn't it?"

He nodded with that strange purpling of his cheeks that seemed to be the blush of an Undine with his coloring. I put a hand against the wall and took a slow breath, the silk tightening across my chest, no time like the present to try one of Bella's tricks. Urchin stared, his eyes all but hanging from their sockets.

"Close your mouth, boy, they're just breasts."

"I'm sorry, I just . . . our women don't dress like . . ."

I narrowed my eyes at him. "Like what?"

All the fire went out of him. "Like humans."

The restraint it took not to slap him had me shaking. He thought I was dressing like a human because I had to? "They would if all they had were pieces of see-through material to choose from."

He swallowed hard and stepped back. I reached forward and grabbed his chin in my fingers. "Where are the cells the prisoners are kept in?"

"Why would you want to go there?"

Tightening my grip, I pulled him closer to me. I had to give him credit, his eyes stayed on my face as they flickered with a barely suppressed anger. Perhaps there was more to him than at first appeared.

"Urchin, I need to get to the cells."

"Requiem doesn't want anyone going there. I can't help you. I'm sorry." He stepped away from me, and I let him go. There was no point pushing . . . fear only went so far when it came to getting what you wanted. I knew that.

There had to be another way to find the cells, to find the ambassadors. But how? I turned in a slow circle, as the thought wove through my mind. If I were thrown into the cells, could Belladonna talk me out of them?

More importantly, did I trust her to stand by me and not leave me in the cells to rot if I went through with my idea?

Only one way to find out.

Chapter 10

The dining hall was empty and a stab of alarm shot through me. Where was Bella? After her walk with Ash, she should have been here, with Requiem. Before I could leave, the same slave who'd come to our room stepped into view. "They went for a walk along the sea wall, lady. The ambassador asked to be shown about and drink in the fresh air."

I put my hands on my hips. "Requiem went with her?"

"No, he is in his personal rooms. He always goes there after midday break."

I made a snap decision. "Take me to him."

Bowing slightly, the human led me out of the dining area and through the circular palace. We climbed down several sets of stairs and crossed a bridge that stretched between two spires before reaching an open courtyard. Ahead of us was a single spire set back from the open-air coliseum. The slave led me into the spire and we climbed a set of stairs that led to a closed set of doors. We had to be a hundred feet above the ocean.

"That is his abode," the human said softly, glancing behind us.

The slave's eyes went wide as he looked past me. The chill crawling up my spine like damp fingertips tickling along my skin had nothing to do with the actual temperature of the day. I turned, already knowing who would be behind me.

"Larkspur, how convenient you are here considering I have been looking for you." Requiem smiled, but it didn't reach his eyes. "Interesting that your ambassador would have two Enders at her side when she is so powerful in her own abilities. What have you been up to this morning, Ender Larkspur?"

I didn't take my eyes from his, not for a second. For the first time in weeks, I heard Granite's voice in my head as if he were standing there with me. *He'll telegraph his every move through his eyes.*

"I've been exploring your palace; it is quite expansive. One could get lost easily."

"Ah. Exploring, is that what you'd call it, now?" He raised his left hand, the swirls of blue wrapping around each finger as obvious to me as if he stated what he was going to do. A small cloud formed over our heads and rain pattered around us. The human slave flinched and backed away, but Requiem stopped him with a crook of one finger.

I didn't flinch, not even when a miniature bolt of lightning danced across his hand. A second flex of his hands, and white spools of electricity danced up his arm and the clouds blew away. Blew away . . . that wasn't possible, unless . . .

"You're a half breed." The words escaped me before I thought better of it. And I really should have thought better of it.

Requiem's eyes widened. "What did you say?"

The slave went to his knees, but I didn't move. I held my ground, bracing myself for a fight. "You're a half breed, aren't you? Why haven't your people slapped you into chains? It's what they do, isn't it?"

He moved around me, closer to the slave. "Tell me something, Larkspur, do you realize the power rumors have?"

Before I could say, or do, anything, his hand shot out and he grabbed the slave by the hair. With a vicious twist, he snapped the human's neck. The crack reverberated through the room and down my own spine. "I would suggest while you are here, you keep your thoughts to yourself."

A flick of Requiem's hand sent the human's limp body flying. Limbs twisted as the slave fell, slamming into the wall. His head rolled back at an impossible angle, and I couldn't look away. His death was my fault, because I'd spoken without thinking. Tears pricked at my eyes. The slave had shown me kindness despite having every reason to hate me along with the other elementals.

Requiem's black eyes focused on me, snapping me out of my spiraling grief and guilt. "We have a problem. I have given my word I wouldn't kill you. Yet you know things you should not. Whatever are we to do?"

Heart beating so hard I thought it might climb from my throat, I shook my head. In for a blade of grass, in for the whole damn field. "Somehow I don't see you as a man of your word. Someone who would kill their own father and poison their sister in order to take a throne that would never belong to him doesn't strike me as trustworthy."

He flicked his hand, white lines racing around his fingers and up his arms. The wind caught me and shoved me through the doors of his personal quarters. The distinct sound of locks slamming into place rang in my ears. I was on the floor next to a monstrous bed, big enough for ten people to sleep in. I stood, but didn't take my eyes from him. Not for a second.

He strolled around the room, hands on his hips as he walked. "Bold. Very bold, indeed. Not something I see anymore." His black eyes flicked to me and a smile curved his lips. "Not that it means you're safe. I wouldn't want to give you the wrong idea." Requiem stopped in front of a huge drawing on the wall. "Do you know what this is, Larkspur?"

Forcing my breathing to even out, I walked closer to get a better look. Names and dates were scattered over the paper, the history of several families by the looks of it.

"Genealogy of your family."

"Not my family. All four families. We all stemmed from the same place." His fingers caressed a name on the far right. The Mother Goddess and next to it, her consort. No name, but his place was there beside her.

I couldn't help but look closer, seeing the places the families blended back together and tore apart. The desire to grab the paper from the wall and study it hit me hard. Somewhere in it was my history, my mother's history. No, that wasn't correct. "You have no one representing Spirit."

He turned to look me over. "Beautiful, fiery, and intelligent. You are correct. There is no history on those who dealt in Spirit. A great disappointment to me that all records of their bloodlines were erased. Though I have heard there is a child of mixed parentage in the house of Basileus. That one of his daughters carries Spirit and Earth."

I stepped back, sure he could hear my heart pounding. I had to dissuade him of the idea. "I do believe you are wrong. None of his children are half breeds. Cassava would never have allowed it."

With a shrug, he turned to me. "She is already here, isn't she? The legends say Spirit enhances the other elements. Makes elementals so strong, they have the force of many. The power of the tsunami was raw, and in it I knew she was here. That is why I tried to kill you. I do not want her to have a protector."

He thought Belladonna was the child of Spirit and Earth. "Then why didn't you just kill me?"

The black silk tightened as I shifted my stance, the muscles in my leg outlined by the material. Requiem's eyes slid up my legs, hunger burning in the black depths. "Because I like what I see when I look at you."

He slid up next to me, and then was behind me before I could stop him. His chest brushing against my back, hands skimming down my bare arms to the tops of my thighs. "Perhaps I can be convinced not to kill you."

Belladonna's words came back to me. To tease, to draw a man out, but not give him what he wanted. That was a dangerous game. I wasn't sure I could do it, but I was going to try for the sake of my life and my sister's. "And your wife? What would she think of your offer?"

His breath whispered across the back of my neck. "She does as she's told. Like a well-behaved woman should." Worm shit and green sticks, his wife was still alive?

The struggle inside my head raged for all of three seconds. I had to keep Belladonna safe. That was my number one job. No matter what that meant, no matter what it cost me. Sex was a tool not every Ender had at their disposal. I just had to use this power the right way.

Before I could make another move, he bit me on the side of my neck, his blunt teeth digging in hard.

I pushed away from him, acting as though his bite didn't hurt like hell, as I turned and placed my fingers on his chest. "I don't do as I'm told. And I am far from well-behaved."

His eyes flashed as I backed away from him, letting my hips sway. His eyes roved down my body, and he stepped toward me, growling, "Come here."

Raising my eyebrows, I laughed at him. "No, I don't think that's going to happen."

Rage flickered across his face, followed hotly by a bolt of lust that left his pants obviously too tight. "I will kill you then."

"Not yet, you won't." I was at the door, the knob was under my hand and I twisted it, forgetting he'd locked it. Damn it. He grinned at me and I smiled back as he approached, fear and anger slicing through me. I grabbed hold of the anger and used it to push past the fear keeping me from my power.

A rush of strength shot through me as I connected to the earth. I placed my palm over the stone door, feeling every connection to the rock, every particle of sand that created it and pulled it apart, broke it down. The door disintegrated under my fingers, sliding to my feet in a pile of gray sand I stepped over. "Be careful who you play with, Requiem. You might find a hook through your gills and your fins removed."

His eyes were wide as he stared at me, to the pile of sand and then back to my face. "Impossible."

I turned and walked away, my back prickling like crazy. I took the stairs carefully, the urge to spin and stare him down nearly overwhelming, but I forced myself to keep walking. To keep moving as if I didn't have a care in the world and didn't feel his eyes on me as I moved away.

The curve of the stairs finally hid me and I slumped behind it, leaning against the wall. Breathing hard, I fought to get my heart under control, as I replayed the scene with Requiem in my head.

I had done the best I could. I hoped I hadn't been foolish. I all but ran down the rest of the stairs and into the bright sunlight. Once I was across the bridge and back into the main section of spires, I finally allowed myself to slow.

I rounded a corner and nearly ran over Ayu. She stumbled to a stop when she saw me. "Ender, thank the mother goddess. Your ambassador . . . you have to hurry."

She grabbed me and I let her pull me along. "What happened?"

"I don't know, she was walking through the palace, her other Ender at her side when she crumpled to the ground. I can't seem to ease the pain in her belly and she cries out for you. I have never seen anything like this."

I grabbed her arm and we ran the rest of the way to our assigned room. As we drew close, Bella's voice echoed through the hall: a cry that made me believe she was truly dying. I bolted forward and through the door. Belladonna lay on the bed, curled in a fetal position as she rocked.

"Bella, what happened?"

Her eyes, pain glazed and shadowed with tears, lifted to mine. "Lark, please don't leave me. I'm so afraid."

I was at her side in an instant, sitting on the edge of the bed. She reached for me and grabbed my hand. Her grip was amazingly strong and the glimmer in her eye caught me off guard. Glancing over my shoulder, I looked at Ash as he paced the far side of the room. "What happened?"

"We were down by the docks, she stumbled and fell to her knees." His face was drawn and again, I could see there wasn't a complete truth there.

"Go to the kitchens. Get us some fruit, if you can."

He stiffened. "I am not an errand boy, Lark."

Glaring at him, I tightened my grip on Bella. "Who can we trust but each other?"

His gaze flickered over me, resting on the bite on my shoulder. "Who indeed?" He stalked from the room. Ayu hovered and I waved at her. "Give me a moment."

She bowed and shut the door as she slipped out. Belladonna gave a long low moan, her eyes flicking to the closed door.

"What in the seven hells is going on Bella?"

"Ash took a note from a messenger. I saw it." She paused and I wanted to shake her but managed to restrain myself.

"And? What did it say?"

She paused and I saw the indecision there. "Spit it out, Bella."

"Drown the flowers."

My heart cracked. I was sure she heard it, the pain so sharp and sudden. "Are you sure?"

Her eyes were serious. "Yes. We can't trust him. Tell him that my yearly is here, that is the pain, and he'll stay away from us. You know that."

As a female earth elemental, we were only fertile for a short period of time, once a year. The time was often marked with severe pain preceding the period of fertility. Usually it happened in early summer so while this was a little late, it was still plausible.

I nodded, stood, and went to the door. Peering out, I gave Ayu a tight smile. "Can you get us some herbals for yearly stomach cramps?"

Ayu's eyes crinkled at the edges. "It's a little late, isn't it?"

I shrugged. "Belladonna rarely does anything when she's supposed to."

A laugh escaped the healer. "Of course. You two are from the same family after all, you should know." I wasn't sure I liked the comparison, but there was no point in arguing it. And I wasn't going to point out just how closely Belladonna and I were related.

Ash came back and I met him at the door, quickly explaining what was happening.

He folded his arms and stared at me, one of the few people I knew who could look me in the eye. "Really?"

"How many women have you been around when they are in their yearly?" I put my hands on my hips, hiding the hurt digging into my heart.

He frowned and put a hand on my shoulder, dragging me down the hall away from the door. "You can't trust her, Lark. Whatever game she is playing, she's going to drag us both down with her."

I brushed his hand off. "She's my sister, and she isn't playing a game."

Ash let out a sigh. "Even the worst people in the world have family. Just because she's your sister doesn't mean she can't be an evil bitch like her mother."

I stepped back, away from him. "How is it you got to keep your weapons?"

He startled and looked down at his gear. "What do you mean?"

"I was stripped of every weapon not long after we stepped into the Deep. You have all of yours. Why?" The tension between us rose, tightening the air, making it hard to breathe. "No answer? That's what I thought." I turned my back on him, but he grabbed me and slammed me against the wall.

"I am here to make sure you're safe, Lark, and I have my weapons because unlike you I have not had them taken from me." His face was a breath away from mine, his eyes blazing with fury and emotions I couldn't pin down. Hot embarrassment and anger made my face burn.

"I am not your charge anymore. I am an Ender. I can handle this," I hissed at him.

"You can't; you don't understand what you're up against. You never have."

"And you're not going to tell me, are you?"

"I can't...." He shook his head.

I shoved him away, or at least tried to. I pushed him, and he returned the favor, which slapped my back against the wall a second time, knocking the wind out of me.

"Stop being so damn stubborn," he growled, his cheek pressed against mine.

"Then tell me the truth."

Again, he said nothing, his silence damning him. We wrestled against the wall, neither of us really able to get ahead of the other.

"Let her go!" A thick silver-coated brush slammed into the side of Ash's head, twice before he did as he was told.

Belladonna stood beside us, her eyes narrowed and her hand raised. She clutched the handle of her brush. "Don't you touch her, Ash."

Ash backed up and gave a curt bow, a red welt growing under one eye where I'd hit him in the tousle. "As you wish."

Breathing hard, I backed away, keeping Belladonna behind me. "You should be lying down, Ambassador."

"Of course, you are right, Ender Larkspur. Thank you." She gave me a smile. Keeping Ash within view as we backed toward our room. I couldn't take my eyes from his. Honesty seemed to be something he struggled with. Who was pulling his strings? Was it my father? Or was it possible that Cassava had her claws into him still?

Slamming the door behind us, I slid the bar over it, buying us a little bit of peace.

I leaned against the door, as my heart rate slowed to a normal pace. An idea was swirling through me, one I was afraid to voice. It would mean the end of whatever friendship had bloomed between Ash and me.

"Are you absolutely certain of the note you saw, Bella? Without a doubt you saw the words?" I slowly turned to her. She stood across from me, hairbrush in her hand still. Though she was my older sister, in that moment she looked so young. A child thrown out to sea to flounder and drown if she couldn't make it on her own.

"I have no doubt in my mind what I saw, Lark. I'll admit it was quick, but the sun hit the words perfectly and Ash couldn't fold it before I saw." She frowned. "But what does it matter?"

That I even thought of suggesting my idea to her made my stomach curl. But what choice did we have? "I think I have a way to find the cells, and take care of Ash in one fell swoop."

Her eyebrows lifted. I quickly explained my idea to her, keeping my voice low. The fact that she nodded, her eyes lighting up should have warned me we were stepping into dangerous territory. But I ignored the fear I was making a mistake. Ash was not our friend—he was not there to help us.

Which only left me one choice if I were to keep Belladonna safe.

I had to get rid of Ash.

Chapter 11

I stood behind Belladonna as she sat in Requiem's private rooms. I was finally back in my vest and pants. They'd been thoroughly cleaned and I was grateful. The slave who'd brought them had been quiet and we'd given her some of our fruit. She'd turned it down without a word.

Belladonna shook her head. "She will die soon. It's what she wants, I think."

I couldn't imagine a life so terrible you were willing to starve yourself to death.

Guts churning, I stared straight ahead at the genealogy chart on the wall as Belladonna spoke, spinning her tale. The story we came up with was simple, and yet I knew it had enough truth in it that we could make it work.

The chart fascinated me, and I found myself working through the families. Some names had been crossed off, others circled. It wasn't just a chart of the families, there was something else going on; I just couldn't put my finger on it.

"Well, as you can see, Larkspur does have a certain look to her that some men find appealing. You do realize that is why Ender Ash showed up on your doorstep? He's pressing his advantage on her. Of course, he's of no interest to her. He's not her type. Weak. Pale."

Requiem's eyes narrowed. "Truly. And why would that concern me, exactly?"

Belladonna smiled and I had to give her credit. I would have faltered under that question. "You have the power here, do you not? Could you put him into your cells? He is not stable and I don't feel safe with him running loose."

His eyes didn't even flicker as he leaned back in his chair. "You would have one of your own Enders put into our cells?"

"Until we're ready to leave, of course. At which point we'll have him moved to our own oubliette. As is fit."

His eyes slipped to me. We had tightened the vest a couple of notches allowing for a bit more cleavage and Belladonna had stitched my pants so that they pulled tightly around my legs and butt. He stood and turned his back to us. "I can have him moved to the cells. But he can never leave. Once someone is put into the cells, there is no coming out."

That was a bold-faced lie. Mako had been brought out. But did we call him on it?

Belladonna let out a sigh. "Well, it is best that for now he is put away from Larkspur. Do you not agree, Requiem?"

He spun, nodded, and scooped up her hand. He placed a kiss on the back of it, leaving a big wet mark. Gross. "Ambassador, if I do this, you will owe me a favor. Both of you will."

"Protecting your guests, that is part of being a ruler. Perhaps you would like for me to school you on the proper etiquette?" Her tone dipped from genteel to icy in a split second.

He grinned at her. "You are the heir to your father's throne, are you not?"

"I am."

Something about his words niggled at me, and I glanced at the chart on the wall. Bella's name was circled.

Requiem didn't let go of her hand. "A beautiful, powerful woman. Unattached. Fertile if my healers are correct."

Belladonna stiffened, as did I. She pulled her hand from his with some effort. "All true. Especially the first two. Something you'd best consider when you speak to me."

"We will talk more of this favor you will owe me, Ambassador. But I do believe, I already know what I want from you. The Ender will be tossed into the cells per your request."

"I want to see him go," I said, startling them both. "I want to see with my own eyes that he is locked away."

Requiem's eyes softened as he took me in, almost as if he cared. "You truly are afraid of him, aren't you?"

I swallowed hard, but said nothing.

"Then you shall see him sent to the cells, Larkspur." He all but purred my name sending a very unpleasant shiver down my spine.

Belladonna and I left Requiem's rooms. She kept her pace even, but under it I sensed her fear. This was a deadly game, one we played without truly knowing where we stood. Or if there was firm ground anywhere we stepped.

Instead of our rooms, I guided her to the docks.

"Where are we going?"

"Just somewhere I won't have to see Ash's face right now. We betrayed him, Bella." The churning in my stomach brought me to my knees. She put a hand on my shoulder.

"He's here to kill us. There are a lot of things I'd lie about, but not that." She crouched beside me.

Who to believe, that was the question. One I had no answer to—not even with all the evidence I had at hand.

"I know you thought he was your friend. Ask him about the note. If he's honest he'll tell you. He should have told you in the first place."

She was right, but I was concerned about more than Ash. "Bella, are you really in your yearly right now?"

A quick nod and a sly smile slid over her face. "I never did have cramps, not even when I was younger. But it's of no concern. I won't let him touch me."

I knew the *him* she referred to was Requiem. "So all those times you had people waiting on you hand and foot?"

She waved her hand, her eyes sparkling. "Well, I *could* have been cramping, they didn't have to know that I wasn't."

Damn, I didn't want to think it was funny, not with everything going on with Ash and Requiem. Yet it was, maybe because it was so far away, and so ridiculous. Crouched there on the wooden slats beside me, I again saw the older sister I'd always wanted.

"Are you going to ask Ash about the note?" Her grey eyes went from sparkling to serious in a split second reminding me of her capricious nature.

As if speaking about him called him to us, Ash strode down the long walk to the docks. His dirty blond hair caught the light, and his muscles flexed with every step. His eyes narrowed against the sun. But it was the figures behind him that caught my attention. Ash didn't notice the Undine Enders, Dolph included, coming up behind him.

I stood and stalked toward him. It was now or never. If he were honest, I could stop this. Tell Requiem I'd made a mistake. "You were given a note when you were here on the docks with Belladonna. What did it say?"

He shook his head. "Does it matter?"

My heart sunk further. "Yes. It does."

I wanted so badly for Bella to be wrong. Why couldn't he tell me it was some horrible mistake?

He waved his hand as if to dismiss my question. "The note was nothing."

I pressed him. "If it was nothing, tell me what it was."

"Fine. It was a request to train with the young Enders here in the

Deep." His words were smooth, but I knew the lie for what it was, could all but see it written on his lips.

I stepped back as he was grabbed from behind. He jerked hard and tried to get to his weapons, but he had no chance against four Enders. "Ender Ash, Requiem is placing you into the cells for subversion," Dolph gritted out the words as he wrestled Ash to the wooden docks.

Those honey-gold eyes found mine. Trembling all over, I fought the urge to help him. To throw the Undines off him and fight our way out. I swallowed hard and took another step back. Disbelief shot through his eyes. "Lark."

"You had your chance to be honest, Ash," I whispered, watching as they dragged him away. Belladonna grabbed me and pulled me forward. "Hurry, or we won't see where they put him."

She was right, but I couldn't un-see his face and the hurt etched there. Betrayal, he thought I'd betrayed him. But he was there to make sure we were killed, so there was no choice. Was there?

We followed the Enders to the throne room where they stood Ash in front of Requiem.

"You've been a naughty boy, following the ladies around when you weren't supposed to."

Ash said nothing, his back straight despite the hold the Undines had on him.

"Nothing to say? Just as well, wouldn't want anyone having second thoughts about sending you to the cells."

Ash startled as if he'd been hit, and Requiem laughed. "That's right, your two compatriots asked me to throw you in the cells. I thought it a lovely laugh." He tipped his head to one side and the Undines backed away from Ash. Belladonna grabbed my hand, her fingers digging in and it was only then I realized I was moving toward Ash.

"You can't. Lark, you can't stop this," she whispered to me.

Requiem waved at Ash. "Have fun."

The floor opened under Ash, a black hole that swallowed him in a single gulp, slamming shut as his head disappeared. I couldn't help myself, I ran forward dragging Belladonna with me. The floor was smooth with no visible lines of how to open it. No way to get in and no obvious way for us to open the trap door back up.

I swallowed hard. No turning back now.

Requiem let out a long, low laugh that built to a crescendo before he seemed to control himself. "Women are so stupid. You had me send away one of your own, a very accomplished Ender from what I understand. All because you wouldn't bed him?" His eyes flicked over me. I backed away, anger, frustration, and confusion building in me like a storm. Dolph stared at me, his turquoise eyes dark with anger. Ash was his friend.

And in Dolph's eyes, I'd betrayed him. Hell, in my own eyes, I'd betrayed him.

"Men are so stupid," I parroted Requiem's words back to him, glaring. "They think everything is about sex and their ability to have it with whomever they want. It clouds their judgment. Amongst other things."

Belladonna tugged on my arm, pinching me hard. "Thank you, Requiem. Will we see you at dinner?"

"Another meal watching you two refuse to eat while your bellies rumble? I wouldn't miss it. I have not had so much fun in many months. I may have to keep you two around after my coronation." He gave us a deep, mocking bow, even going so far as to flourish with his one hand rolling it at the wrist.

We made our exit, and got all the way back to the room before Belladonna let me go. "Why would you provoke him like that? Calling him stupid is not how we make friends, Larkspur." She spoke rapidly about what we had to do next to make sure Requiem believed we were on his side. But the words flowed around me, barely reaching my ears.

I paced the room, my fingers laced behind my head. Ash was in the cells. We were safe from him. And yet, I felt lower than worm shit. Throat tight, I wrestled with myself. He had lied about the note sending us to our deaths. I knew that. Belladonna knew it.

"Larkspur, snap out of it!" Belladonna slapped me, catching me off guard. "We have to focus."

"I am." I rubbed my face.

"You aren't. You're still thinking about Ash . . . mother goddess . . . do you care for him?" Bella's gray eyes went wide.

Fighting to keep my face smooth and neutral, I shook my head. "Not like that. He was one of my mentors. I can't think of him as an enemy."

She wrapped her hands around my wrists, sliding them to my hands, squeezing gently. "I know that look. I've seen it in the mirror. He is not a good man, Lark. Don't mourn him. He would have hurt you in the end."

I jerked away from her, confusion rocking me. Staring at her, I searched for the telltale soft pink glow that would indicate the use of Spirit on her words and actions. I wanted to believe Cassava was behind this, so much easier than thinking my twisted up emotions were my own. But there was no glow of soft pink, no use of Spirit. Belladonna spoke from her own beliefs, and my emotions were all my own.

Jaw tight, I stepped back. "Go to supper, I'm going to get us something to eat."

"No, I'm coming with you. We can't be separated." She met my gaze and arched an eyebrow. "You can't say it isn't safe. I know you're going to the kitchens."

I threw my hands into the air. "Fine. But you're carrying some of the food back then."

Silently, we made our way to the kitchens, the only sound that of her silk dress sliding across bare skin.

We stopped in front of the kitchen doors. They were barred with a thick beam of wood and a heavier lock had been placed on it, a lock I was sure even my thin knife wouldn't do any good against.

"So much for getting food that way," I muttered.

Belladonna slid her hands over the door. "He's trying to starve us out. The same way he's starving his people."

I glanced at her. "What else are we missing?"

She snorted softly. "I wish I knew."

As long as she was talking, I didn't have to think about what happened. The way Ash's eyes had stared into mine, the understanding in them that he'd been betrayed. I clenched my jaw tightly, but Belladonna didn't notice my continued internal upheaval.

"He has some sort of hold on the people, something that makes them very afraid of him. I can't put my finger on it."

I knew what it was, but telling Belladonna meant I trusted her completely. And while we'd come a long way in a short time, trusting people hadn't gone so well for me lately.

But the mother goddess had told me that operating in fear was not the path. Now was the time to take a chance on my sister.

"I know why they are afraid of him, why they bow down to him."

"You do?"

We were out of the main building, the winding, twisting hallways of the palace gave way to the open-air courtyards that led to the water's edge and brilliant white sand beach.

I drew close to Belladonna, putting my mouth near her ear. "He's a half-breed."

She burst out laughing. "That would make him weak."

I grabbed her upper arm and squeezed it tightly, barely managing to keep my voice low. "Not him. He controls two powers with equal force."

Her eyes widened and the color slipped from her face. "The other?"

"Air."

Closing her eyes, she swayed. "That makes sense. The scene above the dinner table that first night. It wasn't the Sylph Ambassador, it was Requiem."

"Yes."

Belladonna slipped her arm around my waist and we walked like that toward the water. "We have to escape, Lark. Sooner rather than later."

"What about Ash? We can't leave him here, and Barkley if he's still alive . . ."

Before I could finish my sentence she was shaking her head. "They don't matter. We have to get out of here while we still can. You may be a bastard, but we are both of royal blood. Our lives matter."

I pulled away from her. "They matter, too. Even if Ash was going to betray us, and I say *even* because I still have my doubts, he is one of us. He is of our family. We don't leave family behind."

We were at the water's edge with the false beach and pure white sand under our bare feet. The heat soaked through my soles. "We need a plan. Weapons first. I can't protect either of us with nothing more than a miniscule knife."

Nodding, she said nothing.

"The Enders' barracks would be the best place." I put my hands on my hips and looked back the way we'd come. Belladonna had taken a tour of the place, I had been too busy trying to find the cells. "Do you know where they are?" While I'd been searching the interior of the palace for the cells, Belladonna had been touring around the entire Deep.

"Yes, the boy Urchin took me and Ash on a mind-numbingly boring tour." Striding out, she led the way.

I jogged to catch up to my sister, wondering if this friendship we had would last once we returned home to the Rim. It was something for my mind to play with other than the guilt and fear we'd made a mistake by sending Ash to the cells.

"Mother goddess, help us," I whispered the plea.

There was no answer, not that I really expected one. There would be no rescue from on high. If we were going to survive this, it was on me to get us out. And whether Belladonna liked it or not, I would get Ash out too. I had to get into the cells in order to find Barkley regardless of Ash. I just had to find a way in.

The Enders' barracks should house the tools and weapons I needed for my rescue mission. At least, that was what I was hoping for. Belladonna stopped on the far eastern side of the Deep and pointed across the water. Separated from the rest of the palace by a narrow rope bridge that hung low over the water, the barracks rested on a tiny island by itself. Made up of white sandstone, the building seemed to glitter in the sunlight. Four stories high and perfectly square, it was a fortress despite how pretty its exterior was. Thin slits for windows, and only one set of doors that, at the moment, were propped open. I frowned. That seemed sloppy. At home, in the Rim, we never left the barrack's doors open.

I shook off my unease. "Bella I'm going to need a lot of gear. Grappling hooks, ropes, and a harness for myself. You're going to have to help me carry it all. Understand?"

"I'm not your pack mule, Lark."

"This is for the safety of you and our family. You will do what I say," I said, somehow managing to keep my tone even.

She glared at me, eyes snapping with fire. "Fine."

I approached the edge of the bridge, eyeing the ropes. The wooden slats floated but as I stepped onto them they sank so I was knee deep in the water. "I don't like this."

"I'm not really happy about it, either," Belladonna said. I glanced over my shoulder at her. She shrugged, but I saw the sheen of sweat on her forehead, the tremor in her shoulders.

"You can wait here, if you want, but don't go far. Alright?"

She nodded and folded her arms over her chest. "Yes, I think that would be best."

I didn't blame her. Getting chewed on by a shark in the dead of night would leave a scar on the strongest of people. I crept across the bridge, the slats sinking with each step until I was in the middle where the water rose to my waist.

"Lark," Belladonna squeaked my name and I froze.

"What?"

"Hurry, just hurry. Don't look down."

Grabbing the edge of the bridge I couldn't help myself and looked over the side. Tentacles with suction cups the size of my head wrapped around the bridge, the wood creaking under the pressure they exerted. A deep, ruddy red they moved and flowed through the water, almost gracefully if it weren't for the fact that they were attempting to pull the bridge out from under me.

Swallowing the scream that lurched in my throat, I pulled myself forward. Bella's screaming behind me was enough for the both of us. But that wasn't what drove me.

Shouting echoed across the water to me from the barracks; the cries of a child's fear piercing my heart. The bridge crumpled around me and if I didn't do something fast, I was going to be tangled into the lines.

I sucked in a deep breath and dove into the crystal clear ocean, praying I didn't make a mistake and get myself killed.

Images of open mouths filled with rows of triangular teeth filled my mind and spurred me on, driving me to swim faster than I ever had. There was a flick of a muscular tentacle slipping around my leg as I gave the final kick before I gripped the edge of the landing. I hauled myself out of the water and spared a glance back. The tentacle creature dropped out of sight, but not before it looked at me, red eyes seeming to burn through me, parrot beak open in a silent roar.

Bella stood on the far side and even at that distance I could see her shaking. I gave her a wave with both hands. "Stay back from the water."

She put her hands on her hips. "Like that's going to be easy on an island!" She did however take more than a few steps back.

Her words followed me as I ran into the barracks, water dripping off me. The scene that unfolded, stole my breath. Three Undines fought on what could only be the training room floor. Dolph and Urchin faced an Undine I didn't recognize. His face was scarred and had been stitched back together badly. His nose was split down the middle and snot flung from both nostrils in a steady stream. His skin was the same pale blue that Mako's had been, though that was where the resemblance ended. Big Ugly was fast, and he kept both Urchin and Dolph dancing as he swung a long line over his head—barbed hooks dotting it—in one hand and a four-foot-long sword in the other.

Across the room under a rack of weapons lay a tiny girl who couldn't have been more than ten years old. Her hair was a deep blue and lay in ringlets over her shoulders. Pale, creamy skin accented the blue of her eyes and hair. She clutched one hand over her side, blood dripping past her fingers. What was a child doing in the Enders barracks?

"Urchin, for all you're worth, protect Finley. She is our only hope," Dolph yelled, his eyes darting to me. As if I were the enemy.

Finley. The princess.

Urchin was blocked by Big Ugly, and I ran to Finley's side. "It's going to be okay, but you need to stay out of the way." She nodded, and I reached above her, pulling down a trident. It wasn't my spear, but it would work just as well.

I spun in time to see Urchin drive a short sword into his father's side. Dolph stumbled away, his hand reaching for his son.

Dolph fell to the floor, a groan rolling out of him. "No, not my son, how could you betray the princess?" He looked to me, raised a hand, and I nodded, a flood of energy zinging through me. "I'll protect her." The words were out of my mouth before I thought better of them. But I knew I couldn't leave the princess to fend for herself, not against two Undine warriors.

Dolph gave me a weak smile. Big Ugly kicked him, sending him flying across the room into the far wall with a heavy thud.

Urchin and his ally approached and I steadied myself. No room for fear, no room to hesitate. Not even for Urchin.

The boy's cheeks were streaked with tears but his eyes were hard. Empty. "I didn't want to kill him. He made me do it. This is all his fault, if he would just do what Requiem wanted and hand her over, I wouldn't have had to kill him."

"Shut up, boy," snarled Big Ugly. He whirled a hand over his head, the long line of hooks whistling as he snapped it toward me with a sharp crack of his wrist. I leapt to the right, one hook burying into my arm and tearing through the flesh. I bit back the cry that rose to my lips, turned on the ball of my foot and snarled at the two Undines.

"Come on, Terraling, come play," Big Ugly said. I slid my hand inside my vest and grabbed my dagger. I pulled it out and with a single fluid motion I threw it at Big Ugly. The thin blade hit its mark, driving deep into his left eye and sending him tumbling backward. Urchin stared at Big Ugly as he fell, his mouth dropping open. Lowering the trident tip, I aimed it at his belly. "Urchin."

His head snapped around, and with it came his trident. His father had obviously taught him well, even if he was still in training. The simple difference between us was that Urchin was proficient with his weapon and I was not. There was no point in trying to drag this out.

He spun the trident as he lunged toward me, tangling the tips with mine. I let him take it from me, the weight of the two weapons forcing him to heave them hard over his head. While he lifted it out of my reach, he was wide open. I darted under his guard and slammed my fist into his jaw—a perfect uppercut that clacked his teeth together with a crack. His eyes rolled and he fell backward like a tree cut at the base.

The whistle of hooks flying through the air was the only warning I had. I flattened to the ground, my fingers curling around the base of Urchin's trident. Yanking it to me, I rolled to my back and thrust the trident forward, catching Big Ugly in the thigh. He roared, his head thrown back, blood trickling from his ruined eye. In the back of my mind, I knew whoever this Undine was, he was no Ender to expose his throat like that, but I didn't have time to make use of his mistake.

His arm snapped forward again, and with it came the line of hooks. They buried into my skin all down my left side, their barbs biting deep. I wasn't going to get away from them this time. A second jerk of his arm and I was hauled to my feet, a scream on my lips. The trident clattered to the floor. I reached for the power of the earth, scrambled to grab hold of it, but intense panic drove it from me. I couldn't stop the whimper that slid through my lips.

I'd failed my father. Belladonna would not be safe. Ash would die in the cells. No, I refused to give up. Refused to give into this asshole Undine.

"Terralings don't belong on the water. They drown," he spit at me, blood mixing with saliva and splattering my face, his eye pulsing. He rolled my knife over his knuckles. "I'm going to return the favor. An eye for an eye, that's what the humans used to say."

He pressed the point of the dagger under my right eye. I couldn't move, couldn't even breathe past the fear choking me. Slowly, I slid my good arm up. I would have to hit him hard and fast if I was going to get the knife away from my eye. I took a slow breath and readied myself.

"Stop!" the tiny voice was filled with a confidence that stilled Big Ugly.

"Princess Finley, don't worry. I will kill the Terraling, and you'll be right after." He grinned, or I assumed it was a grin by the way he bared his teeth.

With a sudden body jerk, the grin faltered, blood bubbling past his lips. His hold on the line slackened, the knife fell from his fingers and I fell away from him, landing on several more hooks.

Behind him stood Dolph, his trident buried deep into Big Ugly's back. He yanked the weapon out and walked to his son, kneeling by his side. A little pair of hands touched my face. "You are not an Undine. Why would you fight for me?"

I turned to see the bluest eyes I'd ever encountered staring back at me. Blue like the Caribbean Ocean as the sun set across it.

The pain of the hooks made thinking difficult, but I managed to keep my voice even. "Because it is the right thing to do."

She nodded and limped back from me. "Thank you." I got a look at the injury on her side, it wasn't too bad, a superficial cut at worst, but it was long. Like a sword had swiped at her and just missed.

Dolph stood and I stared where Urchin lay, shock stealing any words I might attempt. A pool of blood spread around the boy's head and a gaping wound ran across his neck. Bubbles of air escaped him as he died.

"At least he does not know it was his father," Dolph said softly.

I tried to step back but the hooks dug in deeper, working their way into my flesh. "Small comfort to the dead."

Finley slipped her hand into mine. "She is a good one, Dolph. I want her as an Ender."

"Princess, she can't be your Ender. She belongs in the Rim."

Finley stiffened and arched an eyebrow at Dolph. "I'm the princess. And I want her as my personal Ender."

The stalemate might have gone on all night if it weren't for the sounds of voices raised in argument headed our way.

Requiem was one of the voices. "I will have them both sucking my cock before my coronation. One for the power, and one for those long legs."

A shiver ran down my spine. I could take a pretty good guess what and whom Requiem was talking about. But where was Bella? I'd left her on the other side of the water . . . how had Requiem not seen her? Or was she with him? No, she would not let an insult like that go by and stay quiet.

"Follow me," Dolph scooped up the princess and limped deeper into the barracks. Snatching my dagger from the floor, I cut the lines that held the hooks together. As I stood up, my eye caught something I hadn't seen before. A spear on the far wall, not so unlike my own. I limped toward it, and snatched it from the wall.

Stumbling after Dolph, I followed his lead to a side balcony, which opened over the water. Our blood dripped down creating a pink blush in the blue.

"We're trapped here." I may have been pointing out the obvious, but I felt like it needed saying. Dolph shifted the princess in his arms and leaned out over the water. His eyes flicked to mine. "No, *we* are not. But you are."

Chapter 12

Finley shook her head. "We can't leave her. She is part of Requiem's plan."

I lifted my hands, which pulled on the barbs. "I'm not a part of anything he has planned."

She looked to Dolph, ignoring me. "We take her with us or we don't go."

Dolph shook his head. "She is a traitor to her own kind, Princess."

The voices in the main room grew louder and Requiem let out a roar.

They'd found the bodies, but no princess to go with them.

Finley didn't seem afraid or even terribly bothered. "I want her with me and I am not leaving without her."

"And I'm not leaving without my sister," I said.

"The whims of women will surely kill me one day," Dolph muttered.

He held his hand over the water, blue sparkles dancing over his fingers as he called on his power. The ocean rose in a perfect curl. Dolph put Finley into the water and then held out a hand to me. There was no choice. I took his hand and he pulled me into the cradle of water. The salt stung the gouges in my skin, and I fought to get to some sort of surface as the wave curled down around us.

I realized in that moment that Dolph could end my life right there, and no one would be the wiser. My body would sink to the bottom of the ocean and I would be lost. If he would kill his own son, what was keeping him from killing me?

Only one thing. A tiny princess who'd decided I was worth saving.

The water smoothed around us. I broke the surface and sucked in a deep breath. Dolph was already in a small boat, Finley at his side. They helped me inside, and the water pushed the boat along.

"Belladonna was waiting for me on the city side of the bridge." I pointed to where I'd last seen her.

"Requiem could see us, Princess, we have to go." Dolph ignored me and went straight to the helm.

Her blue eyes fixed on my face. "This is your sister? Is she an Ender like you?"

"No, she is an ambassador."

"Do you love her? Is she a good sister?"

Honesty might not have been the best idea, but I was in shock from my injuries and answered quickly. "I love her, yes, and no, she is not a good sister, but she is getting better. And when she wasn't good, it wasn't really her fault."

Finley gave a slow nod. "Get her, Dolph."

A loud snort of frustration blew out of him, but the boat continued to slice through the water. I tensed as we coasted over the deep section between the barracks and the city where the tentacle monster had dropped out of sight.

I stood in the boat and scanned the edge. "Bella!"

A flash of white and she was running across the loose sand. I held a hand out to her and she scrambled into the boat. "Requiem, he went in. I thought you would be killed." She wrapped her arms around me and I let out a groan.

"Not so tight."

She pulled back and gasped as she looked at my body, gingerly touching one of the hooks. "Mother goddess, what happened?"

I raised an eyebrow. "You don't like it? I could start a new rage, piercing every available piece of my body."

Finley giggled and Belladonna twisted to stare at her. Unbelievably, she bowed from the waist. "Your majesty. I see your mother in your eyes."

Damn, she really was good at this ambassador thing. A small part of me hated that father was right about that.

"Where are we going?" I stared at the city behind us, shocked at how quickly it was swallowed up into a fog I had never seen from inside the city. We were headed west which was open water. Not a good idea in my estimation.

"There are Undines who support Finley, but they keep to themselves. We must track them down," Dolph said.

"How long will it take?" Belladonna asked, staring behind us.

Dolph shrugged, wincing. He put a hand to his side and pressed hard. Blood seeped through his fingers. "A month or two. Less if we're lucky."

My mouth dropped open and I stood, rocking the boat. "A month? Requiem will have the throne by then!"

"What does it matter to you?" Dolph glared at me, as if I had done something wrong. What was his problem?

Belladonna let out a bitter laugh. "Requiem's plans go far beyond the Deep, Dolph. You should know that. My father explained it to me before I left. Requiem is one of those who stood with my mother to remake the world as a few Elementals saw fit. We have to stop him."

Shock and hurt filtered through me in equal measure. No one had trusted me enough to tell me the truth about Requiem. Not my father, not Belladonna, not even Ash because it was likely he knew too.

As if reading my thoughts, Dolph pointed at me, then Bella. "You two sent one of your own to the cells. Why should I trust anything you say?"

I reached out and grabbed him by the shoulder. "My father sent Ash to make sure we were both finished off. Do you understand? Ash is the one you can't trust, he was sent to kill us!" I was yelling, but I didn't care. The words poured out of me, like purging a venom buried deep in my body. "He was supposed to be my friend, my mentor. But he's not. He's a liar and I couldn't let him hurt her." I pointed at Bella.

Belladonna sucked in a sharp breath. "You . . . you weren't trying to protect yourself."

"Of course not! You are my charge. Your life matters here, not mine."

Dolph stared at me, understanding dawning in his eyes. "The note, that's what happened, isn't it? I told him to show it to you. The fool is afraid to tell you . . ."

"What? How do you know about the note?" Belladonna leaned forward, rocking the boat.

A sick feeling began to build in my gut.

Cupping his head in his hands, Dolph let out a groan. "Ash intercepted a note meant for Eel."

I lifted my hands, palms out to slow things down. "Wait, who is Eel?"

Dolph lifted his head, his eyes full of sorrow. "The Undine who stuck the hooks in you."

"The note was meant for him? I don't understand."

"We don't know who it was from, but it was going to Eel. He was the one who was supposed to 'drown the flowers.' Not Ash."

"Mother goddess have mercy," I whispered, slumping into the boat, barely feeling the hooks as I leaned into them.

Belladonna sucked in a sharp breath, and then shook her head. "There is nothing to be done for it now. It was a mistake. One we can't undo no matter how unfortunate."

I stared at her, horror growing in me until it flowed from my mouth. "A mistake? Ash's life is on the line and you call it a mistake?"

Blushing, she looked out over the water. "It was not done on purpose. We could not know, and he would not tell us the truth!"

"That is not the worst of it." Dolph's voice held a pained note. "Princess, please tell the Terralings what happens on the day of coronation."

Finley sat up straight in her seat. "On the day of the coronation, blood must be spilled into the water as an offering to the Deep. For protection, for health, for sustenance. The blood must be that of an enemy of the crown. Someone from the cells. An Terraling would make a perfect sacrifice."

I would have moved forward, but several of the hooks where they had pierced my skin caught the slats of the boat and held me down. Frustration flowed up and through me and I let out a snarl. "Get these hooks out of me!"

Finley leaned over and put her tiny hands on my shoulders. "You have to lay still. The more you wiggle, the deeper the barbs will dive. That is how they are designed."

It took everything I had to not move, to lie still while Finley worked the hooks out with a miniscule needle-nose tool found in a small first aid bag in the bottom of the boat. She worked the barbs out as carefully as she could, but the pain was excruciating, bringing me to the brink of screaming mindlessly. Each time my body shook and jerked when she pulled a barb, the others dug into my flesh even more. Belladonna reached over and stroked my hair, untangling knots and braiding it gently. "Shh, it will be over soon."

"You haven't done that since we were children."

"You're my little sister," she whispered, her eyes suddenly glistening with moisture. "I can braid your hair if I want to." The moment was one of intense emotion and pain, and I struggled to know which caused my own eyes to fill.

The waves around us picked up, sloshing into the boat. Salt water washed over my legs where the princess had plucked most of the barbs, stinging and cleansing the wounds at the same time. I hissed and fought the urge to yank my legs away.

I touched Finley on the arm, getting her attention. "How many are left?"

"Two. They will be the bad ones," Finley said.

I stared at her. "The others weren't bad?"

"These two are deep." She touched each of them gently, one buried in my left armpit, the other in the back of my left calf. "I will have to yank them, there is no way I can work them to the surface, so they will tear the flesh badly."

Nausea rolled through me. "Don't tell me when. Just do it."

She nodded, blue ringlets bouncing, and I closed my eyes. The feel of the cool metal under my arm made my heart rate skyrocket as she set her tool next to the tip of the first barb. Belladonna stroked my face, her voice a blend of nothing words meant to soothe a child.

I let out a breath and opened my eyes to see what was taking so long when Finley yanked the first hook.

A blaze of fire raced from the wound straight to my spine and an uncontrollable scream ripped from me. Belladonna wrapped her arms around my upper body. "Hush, hush. It's almost over, just breathe."

Teeth chattering I stared at Finley. "Why . . . do they hurt so . . . bad?"

Dolph answered. "When they are created, they are imbued with pain. Designed to make the one they hook into a useless ball of screaming flesh. That you have managed this far speaks to your fortitude and high pain threshold. I have seen Enders with two hooks in them laid out on the floor, sobbing."

Finley nodded. "You had sixteen driven into you. I don't doubt Eel was afraid you were a chosen one of the mother goddess to see you still standing."

Before I had a chance to slow my heart or think about how bad the second hook would be, Finley had her tool on it and ripped it out of my calf. Muscle and flesh tore and a second scream would have exploded from me if it weren't for Bella.

My sister slapped a hand over my mouth, muffling my cries. "Be quiet, Lark, you must hold the pain in and be quiet."

Whimpering, tears leaking from my eyes, I stared at the sky and waved her hand off. "We are in the middle of the ocean, why does it matter if I'm quiet?"

Dolph looked from me to the ocean in the east and the way his eyes narrowed, the set of his mouth made my stomach clench.

"Because we are being followed."

Chapter 13

Spinning around in a boat was not a good idea, but I did it anyway, rocking it hard. Belladonna let out a squawk, but Dolph and Finley were quiet. Far behind us, the ocean was empty. No city wavering in the distance. "I don't see anyone."

"Under the water, Lark," Finley said softly. "Requiem has sent his enforcers after us."

Belladonna started to cry. "You mean the sharks again?"

Dolph nodded. "Yes. But we are not without our own familiars."

Finley handed me a small vial. "Drink this, it will numb the pain of the hooks now that they are out, and slow the blood leaching from them."

Without questioning her, I took the vial and drank it down. The liquid was sweet, thick like syrup and it clung to my mouth and throat. Within seconds, the singing nerve endings quieted and I could think clearly again.

"You just always happen to have a healing potion with you?" I mumbled, my tongue a bit numb from the syrup.

"Yes. There are far too many dangers not to carry a tonic with us at all times. Every aid kit we have has at least one healing potion. Most have two or three." Dolph said.

I clutched the edge of the boat, the last of the pain from the hooks fading under the realization our situation was about as bad as it could get. We were in a tiny boat, no land in sight, and a pack of sharks were coming.

"Bella, can you reach the earth?"

Her crying eased. "What do you mean?"

I pointed to the bottom of the boat. "Can't you reach your power? There is sand below us."

"It's too far away. Why, can you?" Her eyes still shimmered with tears and something I had never thought to see. She trusted me to get her out of this.

"There is nothing you can do, unless you have a familiar that can kill a shark, and there are not many capable of that." Dolph leaned over the edge of the boat and dipped his fingers in the water. Blue streaks of light shot from his hands into the water in a pulse. Beat, beat, pause. Beat, beat, pause. He pulled his hand up. "We will have some help, but it may not get here in time."

Belladonna grabbed my arm, fingers digging into one of the wounds. "Lark, I don't want to die."

"You aren't going to."

The boat rocked under us with two big bumps that set the small wooden conveyance bouncing back and forth, hard enough to bring the edges to the water's surface. Dolph reached across and gripped both sides of the boat, using his body to offset the rocking. "This is going to be close, my familiar can help, but she has been kept at bay for so long by the sharks, I'm not sure if she'll get here in time."

In time. Before we were all torn apart.

There had to be something we could do. I couldn't just sit there and let the sharks take us out.

My life for Bella's; that was the deal. I grabbed my spear and stood. "How many sharks can your familiar take out?"

Dolph glanced at the water, his eyes unfocussed. "Two. Maybe three before she's killed." I shivered thinking about what kind of creature could take out two or three sharks.

"And how many of Requiem's pets are out there?"

"Six, maybe seven, from what I sense."

Ice slid down my spine as I contemplated what I was going to do. Knowing it was the only chance my sister and Finley had. "Bella, tell Father I did what I was supposed to."

"Wait, you can't go in the water!"

Dolph stood with me. "Lark is right. We are Enders, and your lives come before ours. Lark, aim for the eyes if they come at you. And if you can get under them—"

"I'll open them up like an overripe fruit." I curled my hand into a fist and held it out to him. He did the same, bumping his fist against mine.

"Dive deep, they will not follow us. They are focused on the boat," Dolph said. I nodded, breathing in and out in big gulps prepping my lungs. Triangular fins cut through the water toward us, not huge, certainly not the biggest I'd seen.

"Bull sharks. They're aggressive, and fast," he said.

"Awesome," I whispered. Dolph leapt from the boat, rocking it hard. Belladonna let out a groan.

"Please, Lark, don't leave me up here."

I stared at her for a moment, then looked to Finley. "Princess, you need to be the one to fight if Dolph and I don't come back. Can you do that? Can you keep the both of you safe?"

She straightened in her seat. "No one has ever asked me to fight before. Is it allowed?"

"You have to or you won't survive. None of us will. Use your power, use everything you've got. Do you understand?"

Her face solemn, she placed her hand over her heart and nodded.

I took one last deep breath and dove from the boat. Hands out in front of me, spear clutched tight under my arm, I kicked hard to get as deep as I could as fast as I could—to get past the sharks. Dolph was below me, floating. I swam to him, my lungs not yet burning. With a puzzled expression, he reached out, pulled me close, and I thought he was going to kiss me, giving me air. But he touched the metal hook Niah had pierced my upper ear cartilage with. His eyes held surprise and he mouthed one word: *breathe*.

I shook my head before realizing he held me there, keeping me from going to the surface. He mouthed the word again, touching the earring. *Breathe*.

Niah's words came back to me. "You'll need this going to the Deep. Bunch of mouth breathers there."

Every instinct I had screamed at me to keep my mouth shut, and the air in my lungs where it belonged. There was no time to question if she had been telling me the truth. I sucked in a mouthful of water . . . and it didn't choke me. No time to think about how Niah had known, Dolph pointed up and I looked.

The bright blue water hid nothing; no need to wonder if the sharks were on us. They swayed lazily around the boat. I counted eight. Eight, ten-foot-long sharks with bad attitudes and insatiable appetites. Thank the mother goddess for the syrup Finley had given me. The wounds from the hooks weren't even bleeding—I could only imagine the sharks frenzy if I still had been oozing blood.

Dolph and I swam toward them and I thought for just a moment that this was going to be easy. They didn't see us—we were below them and they weren't exactly looking down. I swam under the first shark and sliced upward with my spear, arcing from the tip of its tail to the base of its mouth, cutting through the soft under belly.

Blood and guts poured into the water as the shark rolled, flailing as it died. Teeth snapped, black eyes went dull, and the gray body dropped like a stone. The water was muddied by the blood and I didn't think about one simple factor.

Feeding frenzy.

The blood set off the rest of the sharks, and they went wild, darting through the pinkish water, grabbing at the bits and pieces of their buddy. I swam backward, bumping into something hard and pointed. I was lifted up like a dancer arced backward over her partner's head as the shark opened its mouth, trying to get its teeth into me. I rolled over its head and down its back, diamond rough skin tearing at me, which added more blood to the water.

Grabbing its tail, I did the only thing I could. I drove my spear forward into the shark's spinal cord. Killing creatures of any sort was not something I liked, nor wanted to do. But these weren't any creatures belonging to the mother goddess. They belonged to Requiem. This would be a battle to the death and I had no intention of crossing the veil anytime soon.

Swimming hard, trying to get to clearer water, I spun in a circle. The water was a mess and even though I couldn't see the sharks, they could still find me.

Without warning, a maw of teeth clenched my left calf, a thousand razor sharp blades cutting into me as the shark dragged me away from the others. The moment slowed as I stared into the black eyes and I realized the shark was not bearing down. He was holding me, yes, hurting me, yes. But biting my leg off, he was not.

I swung my spear around and held it in front of his eye. The grip on my leg increased. Worm shit and green sticks. I couldn't kill him, or he'd snap my leg off. I just didn't understand why . . . until his eyes slid from black to a shimmering violet.

An elemental who could shape shift. These sharks were not familiars any more than I was. I put a hand on its head, between his eyes and the shape shifter's thoughts flowed over me.

Bring her in, don't kill her. Bah. Requiem and his dick need to get their priorities straight. Funnily enough, his thoughts didn't make me feel any better. I knew what Requiem wanted with me, and I would do everything I could to make sure he didn't get it.

My captor swam in a lazy circle and started toward the boat. I counted only five sharks left. Dolph had taken out one, which seemed like too few until I saw him, his body being held by one of the sharks, the same as me.

The water around us seemed to shift, the current changing. I put a hand on the shape shifter's triangular head, picking up his thoughts once more.

Requiem is pulling us home. The black eyes flicked to mine and if a shark could frown, he did, a slight wrinkle forming along what would have been his forehead if he'd been in his human shape. *Can the Terraling hear me?*

I nodded.

How is that even possible?

I wasn't going to explain my ability with Spirit. At least, that was my assumption about why I could understand its thoughts. Not that it mattered, really. Even without his words I knew what was happening.

We were done.

A shiver ran through the Undine shark holding me and his mouth popped open, releasing me as it spun away from me. As if fleeing. I swam free of him, looking back to see what was so frightening.

A black and white body twenty-feet-long cut through the water, bumping past me and clamped down on the shark with six-inch teeth. The orca thrashed its head, tearing through the shark as if it were nothing. The eyes on the shape shifter flashed violet, then dulled to black as it floated to the bottom of the ocean.

The remainder of the sharks swarmed the orca. They darted around her, attacking in pack formation, taking chunks out of her side. Maybe if they'd been just sharks, she could have done more, but there was no way she stood a chance next to these shifters.

The orca's beautiful bright white hide was ripped into, her belly spilling into the ocean. The sharks dove into her body cavity, pulling pieces out while she still lived. I shuddered, grief wracking me for the creature who had traded her life for ours.

Losing a familiar was supposed to be as painful as losing one of your own limbs, and behind me, I saw Dolph jerk hard. As if the blows to the orca were blows to his own body.

Unable to move as shock set in, something below me caught my eye.

From the depths, a smooth current flowed up and around us. Tentacles shot upward, grabbing one of the still attacking sharks. Sucker cups rounded the bull shark, one tentacle on the front half of its body, one on the back half. What looked like a gentle, casual pull ripped the shark in half, his violet eyes meeting mine as he died.

Unfrozen with the thought of the tentacles coming my way, I scrambled toward Dolph. I didn't have to convince the shark to let him go.

Dolph was spit out, and the remaining sharks fled, and we were left facing the giant squid on our own. Dolph wrapped his arms around me, pinning me to face him. He shook his head and even in the water, I could see how pale he was. How much blood he'd lost, not to mention the loss of his familiar. He pressed his forehead against mine though I doubted he realized I could hear him.

The Princess has given us a chance. Thank the goddess!

I didn't have time to really think about what that meant. We were wrapped up in a tentacle that coiled around our bodies, squeezing. Cold, fleshy suckers pressed against my skin as we were slowly lifted out of the water and deposited into the boat.

The tentacle released us and disappeared into the depths. Coughing, I would have thought I would be vomiting up buckets of water as my body struggled to breathe the air again. But that wasn't the case. "Why am I not puking water?"

"The hook in your ear, it converts air molecules in the water directly into breathable air." Dolph slapped me on the back and I waved him off. As interesting as that was, we had other issues far more pressing.

"What happened?" Belladonna clutched at me, her body shivering.

"You tell me. We were fighting and then Dolph's familiar came in, and saved me, and then that giant squid showed up and the sharks buggered off." I looked at Dolph, who lay on the bottom of the boat breathing hard.

Finley sat beside him. "That was Olive. She's my familiar."

Belladonna choked on whatever she was going to say. "Your familiar is a giant squid?"

"The Kraken," I breathed out.

Finley nodded. "I wasn't supposed to tell anyone, but Lark said I should fight to keep us safe." Her eyes sought mine. "Did I help?"

I leaned forward despite the bite in my leg and the pain that shot through me to put a hand on her head. "You did amazing, kid. Thank you. You saved us."

She beamed up at me. "Olive is lovely. I love her laugh."

As if hearing her name, Olive sent two tentacle tips up and over the edge of the boat. Finley stroked them gently. "Thank you, Olive. You saved us. You saved my friends."

I reached over and touched one tentacle tip. "Thank you."

She wrapped herself around my fingers and squeezed gently before sliding into the water.

Belladonna let out a sigh and slumped into the boat. "We're safe now. Let's get out of here."

The water bounced and I looked at Dolph who shook his head. "It isn't over yet."

"That's what I thought," I muttered, looking up to the sky. The water was a draw, neutral ground no one could really control. But the sky?

That was Requiem's to control.

And we were about to taste what a powerhouse half-breed could do when he was irritated.

Chapter 14

The sky above us blackened with a speed I'd never seen. "This is going to be bad. Hang on!" I wrapped one arm around Belladonna and pushed her to the bottom of the boat next to Dolph. "Stay there. Finley, can you help keep us upright?"

Groaning, Dolph tried to sit up, and Belladonna helped him. "Requiem wants Finley dead. You two are about to become collateral damage." The boat rocked hard to one side as if to emphasize his words. Water sloshed in and I fought to find balance by shifting my weight to the opposite side.

Why didn't Requiem just steal the air from Finley's lungs then? It was a trick of the Sylphs. To draw away a person's life by crushing them from the inside out, I should know. I'd been on the receiving end of a Sylph's treatment.

The truth hit me between the eyes with a sharp gust of wind. "He's not that strong. If he was, he wouldn't be pushing us back to him. He has no finesse."

Around us the wind picked up as if in defiance to my words, and all but picked our boat up, shoving it along the top water so quickly, we skipped and bumped. Belladonna fell to the side, slamming her head against the wood. Finley's face was pale, but her lips were set in a thin, determined line. Being tossed at that speed, it wasn't long before the fog surrounding the city rose around us. For a moment the world quieted, and I could believe everything that had happened had been just a dream.

A nightmare come to life that we would wake from and laugh about.

The fog lifted and we drifted into the harbor; no nightmare, this was the truth of what we faced. Standing on the sand, his hands on his hips, stood Requiem, three Enders to either side of him. He called across the water, one hand lifted high. "Welcome home, Princess."

I touched Bella's leg. "Tell him I forced you to come. Tell him you had nothing to do with this."

"Lark—"

"Father said you do as I say when it comes to your safety. Now, do it," I snapped and she closed her eyes, a tear trickling.

"As you say."

A glance at Finley. How to keep her safe? How to stop Requiem from killing her?

"Dolph?"

He cracked his eyes open. The unspoken language of Enders seemed to flow between us and he answered my question.

"I don't think he will kill her yet. He will wait 'til the coronation. What better blood to be spilled than that of the princess to seal his crown to him?"

Finley stood, her tiny frame trembling with what I thought was fear. Nope, she had a hell of a lot more spunk than I gave her credit for. "Requiem, you are a bastard and a half-breed. *My* people will never bow to you."

Our boat thudded lightly onto the sand, throwing me off balance. Belladonna leapt from the boat and ran toward Requiem. "Thank you." He had no choice but to catch her as she wrapped her arms around them. Her sobs were real, I knew that much—I'd heard the crocodile tears too many times from her not to recognize the real thing. He tightened his hold on her, one hand going to her thick hair so he could pull her head back. "Either you are an exceptional actress, or you truly were afraid. I can't decide which it will be. So for now, I will keep you in my bedroom until I decide."

I lurched forward, and three of the Enders rushed me. They circled and I spun my trident out, keeping them at bay. The sand beneath my feet pulsed and my anger made a perfect conduit to the power laying below us. Requiem tsked at me. "Please, give me some credit."

He flicked his hand and the water sloshed forward and around me. I held my breath, even though the earring would allow me to breathe. Vertigo engulfed me and at first I didn't understand what was happening. I was high above the beach, but still looking through water. Requiem had sucked me into a waterspout. I stared down at those on the sand, their words slurred and distorted.

"Send her to the cells. Let her be with the other traitor," Belladonna sobbed out. "I can't look at her." Well done, Bella, I thought. That was a perfect move. Putting me in with Ash, we could find a way out. At least, I hoped that was what she was thinking.

Dolph let out a scream as two of the Enders picked him up, dragging him out of the boat in total disregard for his wounds. That he was even still alive was a testament to his sheer stubbornness. Finley stepped out of the boat and held her hands out. "Chain me, then. You filthy sea worm."

Requiem dropped to his knee in front of her, whispered something I couldn't hear through the sloshing of water, but his lips looked to form the word 'Mary and me.' Who was Mary and why would her name make Finley cry? Requiem looked at me as Finley covered her face with her hands.

With a wave, the water pressed around me, forcing its way into my ears, nose, mouth, and under my closed eyelids until I thought they would pop. I was moving, but I couldn't do anything. Something sucked me down, spun me as if I were in a tornado and then the pressure was gone and I was on my knees in water up to my chin.

Blinking, relief flowed through me as I stood, the water resting just below my hip. My eyes ached from the pressure, but I could at least see. Though, what I saw was hard for my brain to put together. I held a hand out and touched the surface in front of me. The four walls were thick glass, distorted and wavy. Movement inside them caught my eyes. Little tiny fish swam between two panes, oblivious to the fact they were a part of someone's cell. For all intents and purposes, I'd been placed inside a reverse aquarium. The glass was smooth under my hand, cool and slightly slimy.

Slowly, I turned, the water sloshing, echoing in the tiny space. All around me, on the other side of the thick aquarium walls were shadowy movements. Maybe other cellmates? "Hello?"

A voice reverberated to me. "Oh, a new one! How wonderful. What's going on up top, love? The cells are rather boring, I must say." Someone, I assumed the speaker, pressed against the far right wall. I sloshed through the water and tapped on that wall, my mind racing. "Who are you?"

"Pardon me, my manners are slipping! I'm the ambassador from the Pit. Name is Loam. Peta, go over and say hello for us." Loam gave a blurry wave over his head and a tiny shadow leapt above us.

The ceiling was slatted, for air most likely, and set six inches apart from one another, the fish still swimming within the tubular slats, oblivious to the world around them.

But the ceiling wasn't what kept my attention.

A gray and white housecat glared down at me. "I hate Terralings. Let us be clear about that." She let out a long low hiss after she spoke.

I glared up at her. "I'm not particularly fond of cats. They think they are so damn smart. When really they are just rude."

She gave a sniff and she stalked along the edge of the ceiling. "As you can see— " she hopped onto one of the glass tubes, the fish under her feet scattering—"I am the only one able to move around, so perhaps you are the stupid one, dirt girl."

This conversation was getting me nowhere. I let out a deep breath and forced myself not to splash the bedraggled cat.

"Is there another Terraling here? Ash?"

Green eyes narrowed and her tail flicked with irritation. "I am not your messenger, dirt girl."

I held up my hands. "I'm not asking you to take messages. Only asking whether he is here or not."

Loam tapped on the wall. "The Terraling died last night, I think."

His words hit me like a physical blow, and I stumbled back. "No. Not Ash." Grief and shame, complete horror rocked me. How could this have happened so fast? He wasn't injured when he was sent down, and it had only been a few short hours.

"She's crying now. Why did you do that, Loam?" Peta growled. "I hate crying. It irritates my ears."

Loam snorted. "How did I get stuck with you as a familiar? Ah yes, that's right, no one else wanted a useless housecat. Remember that, Peta. No one wanted you."

I latched onto the word "useless" and slammed my hands into the wall over and over. Anything to avoid the reality of Ash's death. "I doubt she is as useless as you! Where were you when Requiem was taking over? Where were you when he was killing his father and threatening his sister? You piece of worm shit! Don't you dare call her useless."

From the other side, Loam was quiet for a moment. "We aren't to interfere. There was nothing I could do."

"That's a stupid rule and we all know it. If you'd done something, ANYTHING, maybe you wouldn't be in this watery hole!" I was screaming, but didn't care. Who would hear me that mattered? A house cat and an ambassador obviously more afraid of breaking the rules than surviving.

Peta leapt from the ceiling and landed on my shoulder, startling me. Her claws dug into my shoulders, breaking through the madness that gripped me. "Quiet, dirt girl. Be quiet, there are those in here we do not want to come to us."

Calm flowed from her into me and my breathing slowed along

with my heart rate. Lifting a hand, I brushed it along her coat, the fur sticky with salt water. "You aren't useless. Don't you believe it for a second."

She sneezed and wiped a paw over her face. "I know I'm not useless. I'm a cat. I'm purrrrfect."

I laughed softly and then rubbed a hand over my face, as if I could clear away the last few minutes. First thing's first, and that was getting out of the cells. Ash's death would have to wait. I would grieve him later.

"We need to find a way out. Who else do we have to work with us?"

Loam laughed. "You think you can get us out of here? Child, for that is all you could be with a belief so foolish as that, there is no way out. This is an oubliette, we cannot reach our powers here."

A shadow moved behind the wall on the opposite side of me and a hand splayed on the glass, palm pressing against it. His voice echoed as he spoke, making me think I heard a ghost, and I struggled to understand how it could possibly be him.

"How do you plan to do that, exactly? A half-breed bastard who throws her only ally into the cells isn't someone I'd think of trusting again."

"Ash?" I threw myself forward, the water slowing me down as I slammed into the wall between us. "How, they said you died!"

"Barkley died last night. He was the one they spoke of. He was too old and had been in here too long."

I closed my eyes and leaned against the wall. A part of me wanted to apologize for putting him into the cells in the first place. But the other part . . .

"Why in the name of the mother goddess didn't you tell me what was going on? Could you not have just shown me the note, you fool?"

"I was trying to protect you!" He slapped both hands on the wall between us, the force of it reverberating into the water, making ripples like a stone dropped into a pond.

"How's that working out for you?" Peta snickered on my shoulder.

"Shut up, cat," Ash snarled, the words hovering in the air. "You aren't exactly winning familiar of the year sitting in a tank of salt water with your ambassador."

She puffed up on my shoulder, her fur standing on end as a low growl trickled over her lips. "It's a familiar's job to protect and aid. But we can't stop our masters from doing stupid things. Like spilling your queen's secrets on your lover's breast."

Loam gave a strangled cry. "You are the worst familiar in this whole wretched world. I hope you are fed to the fishes!"

Peta leapt from my shoulders up to the slats and stalked back to her master. They argued in lower tones, so I only caught a word here and there. Fiametta. Conquest. Cat piss. I shook my head.

"Ash . . . I think my father sent us here to be killed. You know that, don't you?"

A *thunk* reverberated as he dropped his head against the glass. "I feared it. Which is why I came."

I spread my hands over the slick glass. Glass made up of sand. I'd pulled the sandstone door apart, why would the glass be any different? It shouldn't. But that would mean connecting to the earth and I wasn't angry in the least.

But maybe I could change that. "Loam, we're likely to die here, aren't we?"

"Well, that's not very optimistic, is it?" Peta stared down at me from the ceiling once more, her green eyes flashing.

I ignored her. "Does your queen still have ties with Cassava? What are they plotting?"

Behind me, Ash made a choking noise. "You don't think he's actually going to tell you, do you?"

Shrugging, forgetting that no one could see the movement, I didn't answer Ash. "Loam?"

"Terraling, why would I tell you? Hmm? My queen trusts me."

"Obviously that didn't go so well considering what Peta said," I pointed out.

"I hate Terralings," he snapped, and walked away from the wall connecting us.

This conversation wasn't going the way I wanted. I spun around and knocked on Ash's side. "I need you to make me angry."

"What?" His shadow looked up like he was trying to see over the top to me. "Why?"

Sliding my hands over the slick glass, my frustration built, and that wouldn't do me a stick of good. "Can you do that? Can you say things to make me angry?"

"Why would I help you? You had me thrown in here like a common cur."

"Ash, just do it. Please."

"Ridiculous. I was right not to trust you." His words were like a slap, stinging me. "Your father has the right idea. Kill off the ones who cause him the most trouble before they breed like rabbits, spitting out their spawn like demons come to eat the world whole. You and Belladonna, you're exactly the same. You both hide behind your mothers' legacies so people won't think you're a matched pair of bitches in heat."

For just a moment, I believed him, and anger, hot and sure shot through me. I grabbed hold of my connection to the earth. I spread my hand over the glass in front of me, sliding the power through it, breaking down the glass to its simplest form.

Sand.

It fell in a shimmering cascade of clear sand tinkling into the water, fish falling through the air like tiny wriggling stars dropping from the heavens.

Ash stared at me, no longer a barrier between us, golden eyes wide with shock. "How did you do that? How is that possible?"

The anger still burned hot and I turned, breaking down several more walls before the power slipped through my fingers, dissipating with the fury that had gripped me. Loam sloshed forward. "Well, I'll be buggered rightly. This is a rather good turn of events, isn't it?"

Peta sniffed from her perch on Loam's shoulder. "Until the guards see that some of their cells have disintegrated and decide to kill us outright."

Ash grabbed me and spun me around. "How can you even connect with the earth? There is a block put on the cells, Lark. A block that maybe even your father might not be able to break, but you just walked through it like it was nothing."

I swallowed hard, and shook my head. "I don't know, I just did it. Is that not enough?"

Peta let out a low growl. "No, because I cannot shift to my other form. We are at the mercy of the Undines and you just opened us up to them."

I glared at her. "At least we have a chance now."

"Except that you can't touch your power without rage powering it, can you? My first master was like you: anger the only thing she had going for her." She arched an eyebrow at me. Cats and their know-it-all attitudes.

"That's why we're being swarmed with Undines, right now?" I arched an eyebrow right back.

She rolled her eyes and dug into Loam's shoulder. "Stupid dirt girl."

"Pussy."

"Lark," Ash interrupted. "Ignore the cat. She's just pissed because she isn't saving her master, you are."

I turned my back to Loam and Peta. Swallowing my pride, I took Ash's hand, lifted it and kissed his wrist. Salt and a taste of something wholly unique to Ash danced along my tongue. Submission did not come easy to me. I'd never even managed with Coal, yet it was the right thing to do. "I am sorry for putting you in here. For believing you were here to kill me."

He jerked hard, and I wasn't sure if it was because of my words or the kiss. I lifted my eyes to his. With a shake of his head, he stepped back. "You believed I could kill you."

"Why else would you be here when my father told you specifically to stay?"

Loam let out a low chuckle. "Ah, this is funny. You haven't told her?"

I looked between them, a frown deepening as my irritation grew. "Told me what?"

A look of horror flashed over Ash's face that was quickly doused. "Nothing."

And there we were once more. Trudging through the waist-deep water, I put my face right into his. So much for submission. "Honesty, Ash, would have kept us from tossing you in here in the first place. Tell me. If you can tell Loam, you can tell me."

His jaw tightened as if he were trying to crack a nut. "When we get back to the Rim. It isn't anything that is important to what's at stake right now. Which is your life, mine, and Belladonna's."

Shaking my head, I stepped back. "Fine."

"What about me?" Loam stepped forward and I stared at him. The water was above his waist. I looked down. It was well above mine. That was not where the water had started.

"Water is rising. This is bad." As if my words triggered the floodgates, water rushed in around us. Loam floundered. "I can't swim!" Of *course* he couldn't.

Peta leapt from his shoulders to the edge of the cells I hadn't pulled apart. "I can do nothing, Loam." She let out a mewling cry that told me all I needed to know. They might not like each other, but she would still try to save her master.

Like me and Bella.

I swam forward and grabbed Loam, dragging him toward the edge of the cells that I hadn't pulled apart. Pushing him onto my shoulders, I boosted him to the top of the cells. He straddled two of them with ease. "Thank you." He reached down for me and I wrapped my hands around his.

He gave me a funny look. "It's a pity. The queen was so looking forward to your trial, but I believe this will be better all the way around." He let go of me as the floor fell out and the ocean rushed up in a swirling current. The last thing I saw was the look of horror in Peta's green eyes as she stared down at me.

With the floor gone, the water sucked us into a dimly lit holding cell of some sort. I swam to Ash who just floated there. He reached for me, his hands tangling in my hair as he pulled me close.

I planted my lips on him to give him a breath of air.

He leaned into me, his hands coming up to cup my face . . . and I breathed into his mouth. Honey eyes popped open and stared at me. I couldn't help the goofy grin that slid over my face. I reached up and touched the earring Niah had given me.

Floating there he seemed to take a second to realize we weren't done. He undid his belt, and for just a moment, I thought he'd lost his mind. What did he think that touch of our lips meant? A breath of air was all.

Relief, and maybe a little regret flowed through me as he slid a loop of the belt around my wrist, his fingers gentle as they brushed my arm. A way to stay together. That was all. He looped the other end of the belt around his own wrist. I nodded, it would be too easy to get separated. My hair swirled around my face, making it hard to see. I braided it back quickly.

Ash gave a tug of the strap attaching us, then pulled me close so I could breathe into his mouth. . . . though there was perhaps a bit more pressure than we needed. Then again, maybe I was imagining things.

We swam forward, running our hands over the edges of the submerged cell. A thought struck me. The kids in the kitchen, they said the pipe system ran through the entire Deep. If that was true, there should be some sort of pipe leading in and out of the cell to supply the water.

I tugged on Ash, pulling him behind me as I swam deeper, the pressure on my ears increasing with each stroke of my one arm. Awkward as hell to swim that way, but better than being separated.

At the very bottom, I searched the curve of the cell, finally finding what I was looking for. There was a square grate three feet by three feet wide. I slid my fingers around the edges, looking for a grip. Ash worked beside me doing the same. A tug on the belt strap pulled me toward him and I breathed into his mouth. I had to fight not to close my eyes and lean into it. Breathing, this was about breathing. Not kissing. Not touching. Certainly not tasting.

I looked at the grate so I didn't have to look him in the face. I went back to checking the edges on my side. Suddenly, Ash jerked on the grate, his muscles bunching and flexing. I swam above him so I was facing down. Getting my fingers into the crevice he'd opened, I put my feet against the wall and used my whole body to push while he pulled on the grate. With a screeching pop, it gave way and we tumbled through the water with our combined momentum. Ash pulled me toward him and I breathed into his mouth, but he held me, taking several breaths as his chest heaved with exertion.

My legs brushed against him and the ensuing shivers were nothing I could control. I found myself staring into his face, because really, where else could I look when I was helping him breathe? I pulled away first, then pointed to the grate and held a hand up to him. I would check it out, and come back. No point in dragging him through the pipes if there was no place for me to give him air.

We took the belt off, I gave him one last breath, and then I moved as if to dive into the opening. Ash grabbed me and tugged me to him. Another breath already?

Breathing, that's all we were doing. That's what I told myself as his lips slid over mine leaving behind a rush of shivers that wracked my body. He traced his tongue over mine as he pulled my body tightly to his. I gripped his biceps. The muscles under my hands as hard as I'd imagined they would be. I pulled away again, and pointed to the now open grate. Kissing later . . . if that was what he really wanted, but we had to get out while we could.

I swam hard, counting the seconds as I went. There were no turns, which was a blessing, it was a completely straight pipe. Thirty seconds passed and I popped into the open ocean. A glance up showed just how far down we were, the light of the sun a distant thing, barely giving me anything to head toward. I spun around and swam back into the pipe. A minute of breath-holding for Ash shouldn't have been too bad as he waited for me; we were trained for that.

Yet, as I swam, my intuition pushed me faster. I knew something had gone wrong before I saw the blood in the water.

Chapter 15

I popped out of the pipe and stared, unable to believe what was in front of me. Ash wrestled with a deep gray crocodile, barely holding the beast at bay. His hands were clamped over the reptile's mouth, holding it shut as the croc swam them around in circles. Blood trickled from several gashes along his arms, staining the water. Movement caught my eye and I looked up as a second crocodile swam above us. The situation was just getting better and better.

Clean up crew, that was all I could think. The Undines wouldn't want the bodies of those killed rotting and messing up the water.

Swimming hard, I reached Ash and helped him hold the croc at bay while I breathed into his mouth. He gulped several breaths from me and then the crocodile twisted hard, out of our hands. It swam away about fifteen feet, shaking its head. I tugged Ash and he swam with me toward the pipe. I wasn't sure if it was big enough for the crocodiles to follow, but there was a chance. I went first again, this time Ash was with me, his head at my ankles.

We were halfway through the pipe when he grabbed me and we were both yanked backward. There was no doubt in my mind what had happened. At least one of the crocs had fit into the pipe. There was nothing I could do but keep swimming and hope he could hold on. His fingers dug in hard around my ankle and I pushed off the bottom of the pipe with my other foot, clawing and digging at the sides. The seconds ticked by, and Ash's grip slipped, sliding down to my foot.

Air, he needed air. There was no way I could breathe for him, there was only one thing I could do. I slipped the earing off my ear, holding my breath. Scrunching my body, I drew him close enough to jab the hooked earring into his wrist, slicing it through the skin.

He jerked and then his grip tightened. His whole body flailed, and then he was shoving me forward through the pipe. His hand was on the back of my thigh, pushing me. I didn't understand why he felt the need to push me—I was doing fine on holding my breath—until we were out of the pipe and floating in the water. Sure we were still well below the surface, but at least we weren't stuck in the pipe anymore. Ash grabbed me and breathed into my mouth, then pointed at the pipe where a long snout protruded.

Ash's leg bled, and we swam at a sluggish pace with having to stop to help each other to breathe. He slipped the earring out of his wrist and slid it back through my ear. A grin slipped over his face and was gone in an instant.

I knew him well enough to know he was going back to buy me time by putting himself in danger. I slipped my fingers through his belt loops and clamped down, stopping him. He spun and I shook my head. "No."

A flash of frustration slid over him, but I didn't care. We were going to survive this together or not at all. "With me!" I mouthed.

We pushed hard for the surface, though I was pretty sure that would only solve one of our problems. If we even made it. The crocodiles swam out and around us, their tails flashing as they propelled themselves along in a lazy, looping circle. As if we weren't even there. A flash of violet eyes pulled me to a stop. More shape shifters working for Requiem, which meant there was no hope their baser instincts would kick in, even if we were able to manage a distraction. I didn't see any way out of the hot water we had landed in.

I breathed into Ash's mouth as we floated, giving him three breaths. His hands tightened around me, and he shook his head. His eyes didn't leave mine, and understanding seemed to flow between us. We both knew it. There was no way out of this, no way to fight them in their element, with nothing on our side.

Pressing my forehead against his, I closed my eyes and tried to calm my heart. Maybe if I was angry I could connect to the earth. But then, what would I do? What could I possibly do against crocodiles in the middle of the ocean with sand hundreds of feet below and nothing but water . . . I jerked back from Ash, eyes widening.

Sand, sand was the key. If the crocodile shifters couldn't see us, we would have a chance. But how to explain to Ash? I would have to use Spirit if I wanted to speak to him under water. Spirit was the one part of me that would eat my soul if I used it too much. Yet, it was the only chance we had, and there was no time to question my decision.

I grabbed his face and put my forehead to his, trying to get him to see what I wanted him to see. For him to call the sand upward and swirl it around us, creating a fog that could save us. I pushed the thoughts toward him. His body tensed, then relaxed, and he nodded, his eyes brightening.

He held his hand out, and green swirls ran up his arm as he called on the earth below us. So far below . . . I hoped he could pull this off.

The crocs tightened their circle and the bigger of the two whacked us with his tail, sending us toward his buddy. We fought the momentum, but only slowed the impact.

Scales dug into my arms as we hit the cold, armor skin of

crocodile number two. I scrambled along its body and pushed off, shooting us sideways.

And then the sand hit us. The tiny grains ripped through the water, pelting my skin, stinging my eyes. I closed my eyes and held my breath. Ash tightened his hold on me and we kicked hard toward the surface.

Scales brushed against the bottom of my feet and I couldn't help but jerk my legs up—which only slowed my swimming. Ash pulled on me and I tried to help. One second we were swimming hard for the surface, the sand giving us some cover, and the next . . . my right foot was clamped inside a powerful set of jaws.

A sense of déjà vu rolled over me. I'd been here, leg in the mouth of a creature I truly couldn't fight, not all that long ago.

Bones cracked under the biting force of the crocodile and I let out a scream, bubbles flowing out of my mouth. The croc rolled, tearing me away from Ash. Images flashed in front of me. The sand was gone, fallen away as Ash was jerked in the opposite direction by the other croc. I saw the surface, only a few feet away, sunlight streaming down. Then a flash of utter darkness as I stared into the ocean. Each roll disoriented me further, stealing whatever cognizant thoughts I might have had.

As quickly as the rolling started, it stopped and my foot was released. I floated in the water, unable to process what I was looking at, my head spinning from the death roll I'd been forced into.

Deep red tentacles wrapped around me, pushing me to the surface. The water broke over my head and I gasped in a breath, clutching Olive's tentacles as I struggled to understand what had happened.

"Lark, tell me this is a friend." Ash's voice was unsteady and I turned my head toward him. He was ten feet away, wrapped in another of Olive's tentacles, his face pale, gashes across his forehead dripping blood.

"Yes. Olive is the princess's familiar." I ran a hand over the coil holding me. "Thank you, Olive. You saved us again."

She gave me a gentle squeeze and then released me into the water as she released Ash. We swam as she lifted the two crocs into the air, tentacles wrapping around their long bodies and pulling them apart before flinging them away from us.

"Do you think Loam and Peta made it out?" I kept my eyes on the goal of the shoreline of the Deep. The white sand beckoned and all I could think of was how sweet it would be when I put my feet on solid ground. Even the broken one.

"Honestly?"

I shot a look at him. "Yes. Always."

Ash shifted so he was swimming on his side and could look at me. "No, I don't think they made it out."

I didn't think they had, either, which made me a little sad. It wasn't Peta's fault she was stuck with an ass like Loam. He could die and I wouldn't shed a tear. Those thoughts disappeared as my good foot touched the sand and I lowered my hands, slogging through the last few feet of water kind of hopping in order to keep weigh off my broken foot, until I was able to fall onto the ground. Ash thumped down beside me, a groan escaping him.

"Remind me not to visit the Deep again," Ash said.

I rolled to my back, the heat of the sun still in the sand despite being dark out. The warmth drove deep into me, chasing away some of the chill. "And if I do? You still owe me a pedicure from our last adventure."

He laughed softly and flopped a hand over to me, patting me on the head. "Damn, I was hoping you'd forgotten about that." He stroked my hair and I closed my eyes. This, I could do again. But not here. Forcing myself to sit up, I took stock of our injuries. I had a broken foot, bite wounds from the bull shark on my calf, puncture wounds from the hooks, and general fatigue. "Where did the croc get you?"

He held up his right hand. I grimaced at the mangled fingers. "Damn."

Carefully, he turned his damaged hand over, inspecting it. "My thoughts exactly. The healers here are good, but how do we get to them?"

The sound of laughter rolled down the beach, high-pitched and giddy. I turned and shaded my eyes. "I know how." I lifted a hand, waving at the two kids. They saw me and ran toward us, hair streaming behind them in dark green waves. Two sets of green eyes stared down at me. The twins were still far too thin, but they were happy. I smiled at them. "Do you think you could find Ayu for us? Bring her here?"

They looked at each other and then me. "What will you give us?"

I had nothing on me, nothing but the necklace Griffin had given me. With a quick motion before I thought better of it I took it from my neck and offered it to them. "A Griffin's tooth. Powerful magic and protection. You could keep it or sell it."

"Does it heal?" the boy asked, his eyes wide.

"Not injuries." I pointed to my foot.

The girl was already nodding. "I'll get Ayu. You wait here."

She spun, kicking up sand as she bolted from us. The boy bent to take the necklace and I held it out of reach. "When Ayu gets here, you can have it then." They were just children, but I didn't trust anyone from the Deep. Except maybe Finley and Dolph, and even Dolph had killed his own son.

I laid back in the sand. "Boy, sit on that big rock and tell us if anyone comes."

His footsteps were silent as he walked away, his head low and shoulders hunched.

"He really wants that necklace," Ash said, scooting closer to me, his body blocking my sight of the darkened ocean.

"He is welcome to it if the throbbing in my foot and leg can be eased and we can get your hand put back together." I grimaced, swallowed my pride, and asked the question that burned in my gut. "Ash, why did you really come?"

The air between us filled with tension. "There are several

messages I've intercepted lately in the Rim. They all pointed to you and Belladonna being sent here to be killed."

I sucked in a sharp breath. "My father . . ."

Ash shook his head. "I don't know. He might have been in on it, but the messages were from multiple areas. The Rim, Eyrie, Pit, and Deep. All four had messages coming and going. All pointed to you two being wiped out."

That made sense. As an Ender, his first job would always be to protect the king and his heir to the throne. Which at the moment was Belladonna, according to her anyway. "You were right to come. Look at the mess I've got us into. If you didn't know better, you'd think I was a Tracker and not an Elemental."

He smiled and shook his head. "No, you aren't that bad. This mess isn't solely yours. If I had explained to you what was going on, we could have worked together. I'm . . . sorry." His eyes were intense and I couldn't shake the feeling he was trying to get me to understand something else. He closed the distance between us, his lips hovering over mine. "I didn't come for Belladonna."

My heart hammered inside my chest as I stared up at him. No one had ever fought for me before. Not even Coal. As strong as I'd become, as much as I knew I could take care of myself, the thought that Ash would fight for me . . . a curl of heat worked its way through me to my lips. I raised, closing the distance between us—

"Ayu is coming!"

I closed my eyes and leaned my head forward, pressing our cheeks together.

I felt him smile. "Another time. Right now, we have to get Belladonna and get the hell out of here."

"And save Finley," I said.

"No, we don't have to do that." He pulled back from me, a frown on his lips.

I frowned right back. "Yes, we do."

"No, we don't."

"*Yes, we do.*" Forgetting about my foot I pushed to stand and pointed to the water. "She saved us. And I will be damned to the seven hells if I don't do my best to put her on the throne."

Ayu came to a stop beside me. "Lark, I see you've been busy." Her hands were cool on my skin and I forced myself to sit.

"Ayu, thank you for coming."

"You have to hurry if you're going to save Finley and your sister."

"How much time before the coronation?" I let out a grunt as she poked at my foot.

"Requiem decided he wasn't going to wait for the full moon. He's going to marry and get a child in one of his brides so he has an heir right away."

Her words stuttered through my brain. "Wait, brides?"

Ayu's hands were efficient and gentle as she stitched my wounds closed and pieced the bones back together. "Requiem is taking two brides, and if you were known to be alive, he would take you, too."

A whisper of premonition crept up my spine. Requiem's words overheard in the barracks came back to me and I struggled to ask my question.

"Who, who is he marrying?"

Ayu lifted her head, her beaded hair clacking in the sea breeze. "His sister. And yours."

Chapter 16

I jerked to my feet and was moving before I thought better of it. Ash tackled me, his words hard. "We have to plan. You can't just go running into the throne room and expect to get them both out alive. This is the patience you have to learn, the patience of an Ender."

My cheek pressed into the sand and I closed my eyes to get myself under control. Much as I hated it, Ash was right. And he was wrong, too. "You don't even want to save Finley!"

"Will you just wait to hear the rest of what the healer has to say first?"

I nodded, the sand rough on my face. He let me go and I sat up. The twins stared at us with wide eyes and I remembered the necklace. I held it out to the boy. "Here, you did your part. Thank you."

He darted forward, tiny hands clutching at the tooth. Ayu

saw it and frowned. "Why would you give him that? It is a powerful talisman."

The boy grinned and Ayu frowned at him at first, and then her expression softened. "Sting, that won't save your mother from what she struggles with."

Defiance flashed across his face. "You don't know that. She said"—he pointed at me—"it was magical, so did you."

"Sting, what ails your mother is nothing this necklace can heal. I am telling you the truth."

Ash stood and was on Sting in a flash, jerking the necklace from him with his good hand. "You can't let him take this, Lark. It's not meant for the Deep." Sting reached for the necklace and Ash held it above his head, away from him.

"*Children,* stop. I told him he could have it." I stood, took the necklace from Ash and handed it back to Sting, ignoring his frown. "If nothing else, my word is important. I will keep my word."

Ayu beckoned to the girl. "Ray, come here. Why do you really want the necklace?"

Ray shuffled forward, her eyes downcast. "Mama has been having bad dreams. She said the necklace with the big tooth would be the key to stopping Requiem. We saw the Terraling Ender wearing it and thought she could help. Mama is so unhappy when she doesn't sleep."

Ayu sucked in a sharp breath. "Then perhaps we should pay your mother a visit."

Sting and Ray moved in tandem as they led the way, swinging their arms and singing a sea shanty. Above us the moon floated, three-quarters full and bright enough to easily light our way.

"Where do the bodies float ashore?"

"Beyond the horizon forever more."

"Where does the blood pool on the sand?"

"Beyond all that touches land."

Not exactly an uplifting song, and certainly not a children's song, at any rate. I sped up, placing myself beside Ayu. "I am trying to stop

Requiem, but I need to know the rules he is bound by. You can tell me, can't you?"

Her eyes flicked to me and then back to the sand. "I don't know."

I glanced at Ash and he shrugged. I stepped forward, blocking Ayu. "Are you so afraid that you can't even help someone who is trying to help you? Someone trying to save your princess?"

She bit at her lower lip. "You don't understand. I am taking you to their mother, which is dangerous as it is. That will have to be enough."

I put a hand on her shoulder, stopping her. "Then explain it to me."

Ayu shuddered, making her beaded braids tinkle softly. "Requiem is stronger than anyone here. Stronger than maybe any other elemental this world has seen. No one has been able to stand against him."

I rubbed the spot between my eyes, speaking the words as I thought them. "Requiem's a half-breed, so he should be weak, but he's not. Is that why you're so afraid of him?"

Ayu's head snapped up and her mouth dropped open. "He's a . . . mother goddess, that explains so much. He's half Sylph, isn't he?"

I nodded. "Yes. And he doesn't want anyone knowing."

She covered her face with her hands, her shoulders trembling. "I must take you to Otco. There are things . . . things you must know only he can tell you."

Ayu would say nothing more as we walked along the beach, no matter how many questions I asked. She only shook her head and put a finger to her lips. So I followed her example and closed my mouth, but my mind raced as I tried to figure out what was going on.

Requiem was a powerful half-breed who wanted to wed his own sister and mine. As disgusting as the thought of him trying to get a child from his own sister, it wasn't unheard of in our past. To keep bloodlines pure, inbreeding had happened many years ago. But why Bella?

That made no sense. She would give him a child with three elements, two from Requiem and one from Belladonna. A child who would be incredibly weak as the elements warred within it, none able to be first in his or her heart.

Requiem's reasoning made no sense that I could see.

Ash caught my wrist and tugged me back. "Lark, this is not going to help us get Belladonna out."

I tensed and he dropped his hand. "But it will help us stop Requiem, which will make her and Finley safe."

"That isn't why we're here," he said, his voice growing with intensity.

A pure shot of certainty ripped through me, wiping away my doubts. "Maybe it isn't why you're here. But I think it's why I am here. I have to help Finley. I can't leave her to him anymore than I can leave Bella."

He stepped away, shaking his head. "Delusions of grandeur? Really, is that what this has come to? I didn't take you for a prideful woman, Lark."

Those words hurt, most especially from him, and I lashed out. "Yet, I always knew you were an asshole."

Our conversation was cut off as Sting and Ray led us into the poor section of the Deep, where the homes barely remained standing, patched together with flotsam and jetsam. The homes were on the northern side of the open-air market, hidden behind a fifteen-foot retaining wall that hid the majority of the homes from view. Which explained why I hadn't noticed the area before.

The ground was clean though, and everything was tidy if in poor disrepair. Ray waved us forward, into a house that was at best twelve feet by twelve feet, with dried kelp draped over the roof.

The main and only room was lit with candles highlighting the enormous woman on the bed in the middle. She was so large I couldn't see the bed except at the foot where her remarkably tiny painted toes gripped the driftwood railing. Draped in a light blue cloth with patches all over it, she wore no clothes and seemed content to be bare from the waist up. She had the same pale creamy skin as Finley, but her dark green hair was frosted at the tips with silver that flowed down over her chest, barely covering the tops of her breasts. Dark violet eyes flicked over us. Another shape shifter. The Undines seemed inundated with them. "Who have you brought today to gawk at me? I hope you at least brought mama food this time. I told you not to come back without something to eat."

Ash curled up one side of his mouth. I knew it wasn't how she looked; that wasn't our way. It was her soul that shone through like a dark light that had him curling back in distaste. The way she spoke to her children was awful.

Sting tugged at a pouch on his waist, opening it up and offering what he had to his mother. A single oyster. His mother reached over, snatching it from him. Unbelievably, she cracked it with her bare hands and slurped down the contents in a single gulp. "Not enough, Sting. Mama will die if you don't bring her more food. And then where would you be? Alone, alone in this world, you dirty little brat."

Ray started to cry softly. "Mama, please, don't say that. We don't want you to die."

"Mama" sniffed loudly, a noise that reverberated the loose flesh on her body. Sting held out my necklace to her. "I brought you this, Mama. It will help. You won't be hungry all the time."

Her eyes flicked to the necklace dangling in his hands and she tried to rear back from it. "Take it away! Take it away!"

Sting stumbled back and I caught him against my legs. Ayu strode forward, hushing Mama. "Blue, that's enough. You're scaring the children."

I shot a look at Ash to see if he caught that. Not "your children" but "the children." Blue trembled and shook her head. "They need to be afraid." Her eyes flicked around the room and settled on me, narrowing. "You'll be the end of our world. And it will start here. The ripple effects of your actions will cascade through time until there is no one left."

Little hands dug into my legs. "Make her stop," Sting whispered against me. I stroked his head and scooped my necklace from him. I held it up. "Why are you afraid of this?"

She tried to rear back again, but only succeeded in flipping herself off the bed. "No, I don't want to go back into the water. Stay away from me!"

Ayu crouched beside her. "Blue, what are you talking about? You haven't been able to change forms for years."

Blue grabbed at her, dragging Ayu close enough that I was afraid she might try to eat her. "The necklace, I saw it in my dreams. The one who wears it will crush Requiem."

Ash stepped forward and helped Ayu roll Blue over. The massive woman lay on her back, heaving for air.

"We have to get her into the water," Ayu said and Blue let out a moan. "It's the only way, you have to shift. Your creature is fighting to get out!"

Blue cried softly. "He'll kill me, told me if I came back he'd skin me alive, chop me into pieces."

"Enough," I snapped. "Someone tell me what in the seven hells is going on." I looked to Ayu, but she shook her head. Surprisingly, neither of the adults explained.

It was Ray. She approached me, taking my hand that didn't hold her trembling brother. "She is our mother, but she didn't always look like this. She was a princess. She was married to Requiem."

Blue let out a hiccupping sob. "He did this to me. He spelled me to be like this so he could cast me aside."

I stared at the twins. "Requiem is your father?"

They nodded in tandem. Sting looked up at me. "He said we were curs, useless because we could only reach the water and not the air."

The pieces slipped into place like droplets of water into the ocean. My hands tightened on the twins. "And if you go back, Blue? Requiem's told everyone you're dead?"

She nodded. "He said he would skin me alive and feed me to his pets."

I didn't have to ask if she believed he would do it. I'd only known him a short time and I knew he was capable of doing exactly as he threatened.

"And the same for us," whispered Ray.

Blue snorted. "You can be replaced."

My whole body tensed with her words. "That is not true." I didn't know what would happen, and I didn't care. I tossed the necklace to Ash. "Put it on her." I hoped whatever it was would hurt like a son of a bitch.

Ash dropped the necklace over Blue's head and she shrieked, her cry turning into the high-pitched wail of a sea bird. The kids gripped me and I scooped them both to me, one in each arm. They buried their faces against my neck, crying out along with their mother.

Ayu shouted something, but I couldn't hear it over Blue's screeching. The big woman's body shivered, the flesh dancing with her tremors as her screeching turned into full-bodied screams. There was a moment, a single second, when the sound stopped and we all stared at Blue who stared back at us.

The moment passed and a spurt of water shot out of her belly, like a spout under pressure finally unstopped. She clamped a hand over it, but another shot out beside it. More and more, water shot out of her, soaking the room and everyone in it. I stumbled back, holding the kids tightly. Maybe the whole necklace thing had been a bad idea.

A bellow erupted out of Blue and with it, her body tore apart, water slamming into us like a tidal wave.

The kids and I were swept out the door and sent tumbling down the street like a crocodile on a belly slide. We slid to a stop against a building across the way. With all the shrieking that had gone on, I'd expected Undines to come running. But there was nothing, just silence.

"Is Mama . . . dead?" Sting gulped, his eyes a mixture of hope and fear.

"I don't know." I stood and helped them to their feet. The door to their home flung open and a svelte, tall woman stood there, violet eyes flashing as she saw me. The necklace hung between her large breasts, bouncing between them as she stalked toward us.

"You, you did this to me."

I pushed the kids behind me. "I did. And I'd do it again."

Maybe not the best choice of words, but it was the truth. And as I was learning, the truth was not to be trifled with.

Blue raised her hands, deep lines of magic running from her fingers to her elbows. I saw her intent and I stood there, slack-jawed in shock. She couldn't possibly mean what I thought she did. Did she?

The magic slammed into me. Apparently she did.

Chapter 17

Blue's power dropped me to my knees. There was nothing gentle about the magic, yet it healed me, the bones in my foot knitting together, the wounds from the hooks closing over. Shivering, I stared up at her. "I thought you were going to kill me."

"My magic can do both. I can heal a wound or rip it open. But Ayu said that bastard of a husband of mine is going to marry two women. Starving us all is one thing, but this?" She flipped her hair back, exposing her breasts further. "Completely unacceptable. If anyone is going to rule, it will be me. So I will help you stop him." She yanked the necklace off and tossed it to me. "You are the only one with a chance of killing him, Larkspur, small though that chance might be, it is there."

Well, that was comforting. "Any idea how I might make it happen?"

She waved at me. "Enders. So useless when it comes to

manipulation and planning. I will go to Requiem and request to be re-instated at his side. Of course, he will take me and then you will come to the throne room and challenge him to a duel."

Ash cleared his throat. "That seems too easy. What aren't you telling us?"

She put a hand to her chest, splaying her fingers as her eyes widened. "Whatever do you mean?"

"He means you have something up the proverbial sleeve," I pointed out.

Perhaps we would have had more of a discussion, but a sudden shout up the street startled us all. Blue reached for the twins, dragging them close. "Come, children, we are going to visit your father."

We ducked behind a house as Blue dragged Sting and Ray toward the voices. Castle guards swept around the corner, lowering their tridents upon seeing them. "Drop your weapons. Do you not recognize your queen when you see her?" Blue spit the words at them and I had to admit, she sounded queenly. Or at least, like the only queen I'd ever known.

The guards surrounded them and escorted them up the road, Blue snapping at them every few feet.

Sting and Ray both glanced back and the look in their eyes sliced me open. Hollow, empty, as if they knew what was coming for them.

Ash grabbed me and held me back. "No, you can't. We can't help any of them if we're caught now. We have to figure out what the hell is going on with Requiem before we face him."

I turned, surprise filtering through me. "So you're with me now?"

"Do I have a choice? The only way to get us all out of here is to convince Requiem to let us go. And that isn't going to happen, is it? So we have to kill him."

Ayu shook her head. "You speak true. There is no way he will let you go. Come, quickly."

The three of us scuttled through the lower levels of the Deep until we reached the dividing line between the rich and the poor. Not a lot more activity, but it was still busier than the poor section.

Ayu dragged us into a side ally. "You are too recognizable. Wait here, I will come back with Octo."

Before we could protest, she was gone.

"I hope you are trusting the right people," Ash said softly. I leaned against the wall, the sandstone rough against my skin. I looked down at my clothes, what was left of them. My vest had been torn in the middle, exposing my belly to the cool night air. He reached over and touched me, his fingers light across my sensitive skin. A shiver trembled through me and I looked up at him.

"So do I."

His jaw ticked and he backed a few steps.

I let out a slow breath. "The pipe system runs through the whole city. It's how the kids were breaking into the kitchen to snatch food. Maybe we could utilize the pipes, swim through them to get to the throne room without being stopped."

"And do you know the layout of the pipes? I know you can breathe the water with that hook in your ear, but I can't. You would have to go in alone."

"I know." But already I knew that wouldn't work. There was no way I could learn the ins and outs of the pipe system in the time we had.

He stared hard at me, as if he would say something else. But he finally shook his head and looked away. "Someone's coming."

I crouched low, and Ash did the same as we waited. There was no way of knowing who was coming, or if we would have to fight. Relief flowed through me as Ayu's voice floated down to us. "Please, you spoke with the Terralings' ambassador. Will you at least advise me on this?"

A deeper voice, one vaguely familiar answered her. "Healer, what I spoke of with my old friend was inconsequential to what is happening now."

I stood as they rounded the corner. The old man who'd helped me find the kitchens in what seemed like a lifetime ago stared at me in surprise. "You're Octo?"

"Ah, Ender Larkspur. I see you have survived the cells."

Ash stood and Octo blinked rapidly. "It seems we have an epidemic of survivors. How wonderful."

"You spoke with Belladonna, how is she?" All I wanted to know was that she was alive and we weren't too late.

Octo shook his head slowly and my heart sank. "I was friends with the previous ambassador, Barkley." He paused as if gathering his thoughts and a huge sigh slipped out of him. "Barkley figured out what was happening long before any of us did." The old man stuck his hand into his vest and rooted around, finally pulling out a thick bundle of papers. "It was all I managed to save, but in it I do believe you will see what Requiem plans. Not that anyone will believe you. I certainly didn't believe it when I saw what was laid out."

His hand shook as he passed me the papers. I took them, flipping through them quickly. Family trees were drawn for all four elemental families. Exactly like those on the walls of Requiem's room. I frowned at them, handing some to Ash. "Genealogy?"

Octo reached out and tapped the papers. "Yes, it is very important to Requiem, as you may have noticed. He believes he has the key to creating something we all thought impossible."

I turned the final sheet over to see a single sentence scratched into the paper. I read it out loud. "A child will come, who will control all elements, and he shall rule all the families."

The words sunk into me, completing the puzzle I'd been putting together since we'd arrived. "He means to have a breeding program, doesn't he? He's trying to get a child who carries all the elements with equal strength in all of them."

Ayu lifted her hands, as if to stop me. "That isn't possible. One family has been wiped out, destroyed. Therefore, he could never make this happen."

Spirit—that was what she meant—Spirit had been wiped out according to the other families. Ice slid down my spine, and I worked to calm myself as I stared at the papers. It was not common knowledge that my mother carried Spirit. But if Requiem knew Spirit could boost another element power, he might have guessed that whoever had set off the tsunami did so with more power than they should have.

And he knew a child within our family carried Spirit—worse, he thought it was Belladonna.

"Requiem thinks Belladonna is a half-breed like him," I whispered. "He thinks she is powerful with her connection to the earth because she carries Spirit with her as well. She doesn't, but he believes she does." Damn me and the anger that caused the tsunami.

The two Undines and Ash stared at me as if I were speaking gibberish. "You don't know that."

"I do. It explains so much. Why he was careful with her, why he didn't just have her killed. He had her marked from the beginning." I closed my hands over the papers, crumpling them.

But how . . . how could he even begin to suspect, who would tell him that a child of the earth would come and have Spirit tied to her too?

"Cassava," I breathed her name and beside me, Ash stiffened.

"What has she to do with this?"

My words were no prophecy, they were a certainty that rode me hard. "Cassava knew Father would have to get me out of the Rim if I were to survive. How do we know she didn't plant a suggestion before she left? It would seem natural to remove me. She had to know about Requiem as this was happening before she was ousted.

"Which meant he might have approached her even, looking for a half-breed who fit his breeding requirements. Father sent me and Belladonna, but Requiem would only see Belladonna as a possible mate, since she is the heir to our family's throne." I sucked in a big breath and Ash wrapped his arms around me, pulling me to his chest.

"You are grasping at splinters, Lark. You don't know if any of that is true. Guesses are not the same as fact."

I wrenched myself out of his arms and shook the papers in his face. "It's here! Don't you see? Barkley *knew.* He knew what was going on. He would have sent the information to my father who was controlled by Cassava."

Ash put his hands on his hips and bowed his head. His silence stung me, as if a thousand tiny biting gnats drove tiny teeth into the small piece of trust I still had for him.

He raised his head. "I was wrong before. I was wrong not to trust you."

Hope flared in my chest and I waited, breathless. "I'm not wrong about this. I know it."

Slowly, he nodded, but the words he said stunned me. "Lead. I will follow."

I swallowed a lump in my throat. "We have to get to the throne room."

Such a simple statement, and yet, accomplishing it would be anything but.

Octo gave me a smile. "Ah, well, I think I can help you there."

We all turned to face him and I couldn't help asking. "What happened to being afraid of Requiem like everyone else? You even said you wouldn't give me your name for fear of him finding out you spoke with me."

He raised his eyebrows, the gray fluff blowing in the breeze like the under feathers of a goose. "And if he knew you were speaking to the one person who might know what he was truly doing? What do you think he would have done to us both then? It would have done none of us any good to have him know. Pick your battles, young one."

Octo made a good point. Several actually. As he leaned against the wall, he thumped his walking stick on the pebbled road, a shell cracking under the tip. "While I believe old men should leave the fighting to younger ones, I'm not above taking one last shot at making things right. Perhaps I can make the memory of my friend shine a little brighter if I do this." His eyes swelled with grief and love, and the truth hit me square between the eyes.

I took his hand. "I'm so sorry you lost him."

Octo squeezed my fingers. "He was a good man, a brilliant man. He tried to tell me and I . . . I didn't believe him. We fought about it, and he left. I never saw him again."

I remembered him wandering the same halls as me, the hall with the supposed secret entrance to the cells. "You were looking for a way into the cells too, weren't you?"

A bitter laugh escaped him. "Yes, but I didn't have the gumption to be thrown in with him as you two did. Too much fear for too long in these old bones. But no more. I will help face down Requiem and whatever comes will be my reward or punishment."

His earlier words reverberated in my head. Pick your battles. Requiem had shown us how very powerful he was and that he wasn't afraid to use that power. How many more lives would be wiped out if we tried to face him without a solid plan?

The chance was too high that he would kill us all. And seeing how we were completely outnumbered, I wasn't willing to take that chance. My job was still first and foremost to get Belladonna to safety. The only way to do that was to keep my own skin, and Ash's, intact.

Folding the papers, I smoothed them out and handed them to Ash. "We just need to get Finley and Belladonna. That's the plan. We get them out and we get out of the Deep. We'll wait 'til after the wedding ceremony." Which would make it near dawn.

Ayu gasped. "You would let him wed your sister?"

I didn't get a chance to answer her. Ash did it for me. "It makes sense. He won't be expecting us after the ceremony. He'll be waiting on us prior to it, or during."

I looked at him. "You think he knows we survived?"

"When his shape shifters don't come back, he'll go looking. Or send more of his lackeys to make sure we're dead."

Octo and Ayu looked at each other and then me. "You won't try to kill him?"

I shook my head. "I'm an Ender. I have no right to his life, and while I think he should die, I don't want to risk anyone else's life to make it happen. Certainly not my sister's, and not Finley's, either."

We spoke a little longer, to clear up the details. Ayu would go to Requiem and make sure the two girls were "healthy" enough for being wedded and bedded. She would tell them we were coming for them, to stay strong. Octo would try to get word to my father. According to the old Undine, Requiem planned to go old school, marrying his two brides, and then sending them to his bedroom to wait on his pleasure. He would take part in the revelries and Octo would do his best to get him stinking drunk and keep him away as long as possible.

Ash and I would break into Requiem's private quarters, wait for Belladonna and Finley, at which point we would extract them. Ayu would make sure there was a skiff waiting for us.

Such straightforward plans.

Yet my stomach rolled with anxiety as we waited. Standing in the darkness, the clear weather turned as if in tandem with my fears. The night sky clouded over and the wind picked up. Sharp, cold air snapped along Ash and me as we waited in the alley.

"I've got a bad feeling about this," I whispered as the first rumble of thunder boomed into the night. Ash's fingers brushed against mine.

"Don't say that, I'm starting to look forward to my pedicure."

Laughing softly, I shook my head. "Damn, I was hoping you'd forgotten."

His eyes shone in the darkness, as if lit from within. "Never."

Chapter 18

From our hiding spot, we heard the drums that signified the start of the wedding ceremony. My palms were sweaty and my heart rate soared as I strained to hear the words that would bind Belladonna and Finley to Requiem. I kept reminding myself when he was dead, the vows would be nullified.

Octo had managed to get us a few weapons—two daggers for me, and a mid-length sword for Ash—and made sure the boat Ayu secured for us was tied up on the western side of the Deep, closest to land. Closest to where we could use the armband again and Travel back to the Rim and safety. I touched the armband for the first time in a long while. That it was still there after all that happened shocked me.

Ayu had slipped away, her shoulders tight and hunched. We knew as she did that there was a very good chance Requiem would wonder why she was checking on the two girls. Even though she was a healer, it wasn't common practice to certify the health of a prospective bride—or in this case, brides.

Requiem's voice boomed over everyone else's, but still, the words were muffled and I couldn't make out a thing he was saying. The only good thing about hearing his voice was we knew he was busy. Even if he was marrying his own sister and mine. From our high perspective outside Requiem's personal quarters, I stared across the courtyard at the twinkling lights and people wandering in the throne room that was somehow opened to the sky.

"Do you think Blue was able to stop him?" I glanced at Ash while I hopped in place, my nerves jangling to get moving. We had a long climb ahead of us and I didn't want to burn out early, but I was jittery. The wall in front of us was easily the height of a redwood from back home, but that wasn't what was bothering me. No, it was the fact that if we were caught, there would be no cells waiting for us. Requiem would kill us and be done with it.

Ash reached out and got a grip on the wall, pulled himself up, and dug his toes into crevices I couldn't see. His muscles flexed in his thighs as he clung to the wall. "If Blue had managed to cause even a hitch in his plans, there wouldn't have been any drums. I'd be surprised if she is still alive."

Even though I'd already thought the same thing, I had hoped Blue had at least been able to slow Requiem down. Tucking my fingers into a crack in the wall, I pulled myself up and felt around with my toes for a ledge to push from. The tiniest of openings beckoned to my right foot and I jabbed it against the sandstone with maybe more force than I needed. Then again, I didn't really want to fall.

No matter how strong we were, or how fast we healed, that didn't mean I wanted to feel the pain of a fall like this and deal with the recovery. Who was I kidding, if I fell, there would be no recovery; Requiem would end my life. Or worse, try to marry me too.

Our backs were to the ocean as we climbed. Was there a door and stairway into Requiem's personal sanctum? Of course there was. And it was heavily guarded and not worth the bloodshed when we could climb. Bad enough that we had to leave that way. We didn't want to alert Requiem and his lackeys until we absolutely had to.

My right hand slipped off my next grip and I hung in space from my left hand for a split second before I managed to dig my toes into the wall. Breathing hard, I dared a glance down. We weren't even halfway up yet and I was struggling. So much rode on us doing this exactly right. Lives hung in the balance, and I did not want to screw this up.

Above me, Ash paused and glanced down. I gave him a nod, knowing how well voices carried over the water.

Fifteen minutes of climbing and my whole body was a tense bag of muscles and tendons. Ash reached the balcony and pulled himself over the railing. He disappeared into the room, the curtains fluttering around him.

"Thanks for the hand," I breathed out as I reached for the next handhold. The pain that shot through my right foot made me hiss. A shell embedded into the wall stuck out far enough to slice me open, but not far enough to use as a grip. The blood on my foot made using it impossible to grip.

Inside the room came a thump and a gargle of a strangled cry. Adrenaline pumping, I tried to scramble up the wall, which only caused me another cut on the bottom of my foot from the same damn shell.

A second thump and the curtains blew out as if bodies were being tossed around inside. Gritting my teeth, I knew there was only one way I was getting up there fast enough to help.

Gauging the distance between me and the bottom of the balcony there wasn't much choice. I couldn't wait for Ash if he was getting his ass handed to him; my muscles were giving up, and one foot down didn't leave me the control I needed.

I took a deep breath, coiled in on myself and leapt for the bottom of the railing. The air around me seemed to caress my face and arms as I stretched for the rail, every muscle pushed to its limit.

My fingers hooked the edge of the flooring and I hung for a

moment, shocked when I realized I'd made it. Pulling myself up, I hooked a leg over the edge, stood and hopped the banister.

The gauzy curtain swirled outward and a figure moved behind it. I crouched, hands going to where the daggers rested at my belt. "Ash?"

A figure moved closer, but didn't answer. I shifted the two daggers out, one in each hand with the blades flat against my wrists. As the figure parted the curtain, I leapt forward, seeing the blond hair and honey eyes too late. Ash caught me, his hands going to my butt as he stumbled back, trying to gain his balance under our joined momentum.

"What are you doing?" He came to a stop and dropped me to my feet. The skin under his hands burned as if he'd slapped me leaving a trail of tingles all the way down my legs.

"I thought you were hurt," I whispered, pointing a knife at him. "When someone calls your name, you should answer."

"Help me drag his body to the balcony," he said.

I put my daggers away and grabbed one of the intruder's feet. "One of the guards? Won't they notice he's missing?" This rescue mission was going sideways already.

"No, I think he was a thief. See the tools? He was the one who cut those grips in the wall. He came up the same way to rob Requiem while he was at his wedding."

I stared down at the red hair. "He's a Salamander."

"That, he is."

I frisked the dead thief as the implications raced through my mind. Fiametta must have sent him, whoever he was. A bag of tools was one thing. But it was the paper that he'd taken that caught my eye. The genealogy Requiem was obsessed with. I took it and tucked it into my vest. Ash gave me a look but said nothing. We dragged the thief's body to the balcony and pushed it to the side.

Fiametta wanted Requiem's bloodline information? Was it truly that important?

Before I could wonder further, Ash lifted a finger to his lips and pointed to the door. The heavy clunk of multiple footsteps climbing the stairs reached us. We stepped back onto the balcony, moving to either side without even speaking to one another.

The curtain blew out around us as the air pressure in the room shifted.

"Princess, I'm sorry."

Finley spoke, her voice sharp. "Get out. None of you are worth my favor. Not one." Requiem wasn't with her, which was good. Except I didn't hear Bella. Where in the seven hells was she?

The footsteps retreated and then the door clicked shut. I motioned at Ash to stay as I slipped back into the room.

A cloud of light blue material sat in the middle of the room, dark blue hair piled high on top of it like some sort of living cupcake. "Finley."

She spun around, her eyes going wide and filling with tears. Stumbling over her poofy skirts, she ran toward me. "Lark, you're alive! Requiem laughed at the ceremony, he said you would show up there or not at all. But Ayu said you would come for me. I wanted to believe her, but I was so scared. I couldn't get Olive close enough to Requiem. I wanted to fight, I did!"

I smoothed her hair, plucking out the pins so as to let the monstrosity down. "I almost did come to the ceremony, but that would have been a disaster. My friend, Ash talked me out of it." He stepped out from behind us and gave a bow to her. "Princess."

Her eyes widened as she looked him over. "He's another Ender, like you?"

"Yes. Finley, where did Requiem take Belladonna? We're going to get her and you and escape. Someone else will have to deal with Requiem." The words sounded cowardly, even to me, even knowing that Requiem would kill us all without a single qualm.

Finley pointed below us. "She's still at the party. She doesn't look well, Lark. She's been very sick since you've been gone."

Ash let out a hiss. "Poison."

We had to hurry. We'd been separated less than twelve hours, but I didn't know how long a poison would take. The only thing I could think was Requiem believed if he married Belladonna, and then killed her, he could take my father's throne. Icy anger crackled through me.

Requiem was about to find out there was more than one way to flay a shark.

"Finley, how many guards are there between here and the . . . party?" I held her hands tightly and didn't look away while her eyes grew thoughtful.

"Three in the tower, two at the front gate. That's all I saw. Lark, we can get to her. We can, I think he put her in a small holding room where she can be sick on her own. I can get you there." Her eyes were bright with hope. I looked to Ash for guidance.

"We don't have a choice," I said.

"I know, that doesn't mean I like it." He strode to the door and peeked out. "The stairs are wide enough we can fight side by side. Silent and fast, that's how we're doing this."

I took Finley by the hand. "You stay behind us, understand?"

She bobbed her head. "I knew you would come for us."

I touched her head and then stood and moved to Ash's side. "Ready."

He opened the door and we descended the stairway side by side in a fast crouch. The first guard didn't even turn around, didn't even suspect he was about to die. I clamped one hand over his mouth and twisted his neck, spinning his body out so Ash could drive his sword through the guard's heart.

Guard two and three were equally oblivious to us. At the bottom of the stairs, I jogged back up half a flight to where Finley waited. Her face was pale as she stared at the headless corpse of guard number three. "He was always nice to me, even when Requiem wasn't." A tear trickled down her cheek.

"I'm so sorry that we have to do this, Finley." I reached out and brushed the tear away. She nodded. "I know. That's why you are so good. You don't want to hurt people. You want to help them."

Guilt gnawed at me. That may have been true, but I was about to kill another person to get to Bella. Ash motioned me to him. I gave Finley one last touch on the top of her head, then hurried down the stairs to Ash's side. He put his mouth right against my ear.

"Two guards. You go left."

I nodded and adjusted my grip on the two daggers, already seeing the move in my head. Overhand downward strike with my right hand driving the blade into the neck, left-handed dagger would come in hard to the kidney. The doors opened inward, and we yanked them fast, leaping through the space.

True to what Finley remembered, there were only two guards.

But they were both Enders.

My first blow to the neck bounced off the spinning machete that deflected it. My left-handed blow did connect, but not in the kidney. The dagger tore through the muscles in his side, pulling a grunt from the Ender, but nothing more. I let myself unbalance and go to my knees. The Ender, Carp I thought his name was, loomed over me, sneering. "You Terralings are so damn weak."

I hung my head and didn't look up as I swung with my right hand again, cutting through his hamstring. He went down with a surprised yowl that made me cringe. At least the music and laughter from the party was loud enough that he might not be heard.

Then there was no thought for how loud or quiet we were. Carp came at me like an enraged walrus, limping but still driving me back with the machete's longer reach. The snarl on his lips said it all. He was furious. I flipped the right dagger up, spun it, caught the handle, and threw it at him. The blade buried deep into his left cheek. He gagged and yanked it out, slicing his face open in the process.

I didn't wait for him to catch his breath. Leaping, I body slammed him, driving us both to the ground. Not unlike what I'd planned for Ash when I'd climbed onto the balcony. Except Ash had been ready for me. Carp was not.

I landed on his chest and we hit the pebbled road hard. Several of his ribs cracked underneath our combined weight and landing force, the snap of them loud enough to leave no doubt they were broken clean through. I whipped my second dagger out and swept it toward his heart.

"Please don't kill me, I don't stand with Requiem," he bubbled out past the blood and fear. His eyes pled with me, lips smeared red.

"But you do, or you would not have allowed me to be taken. You would have fought for me if you stood with me," Finley said behind me. I held the dagger steady, the point at the perfect angle that a quick thrust would send it home.

"Princess," he whispered. "He threatened to kill us all."

"Cowards. It has taken two Terralings you said were weak and useless to show me bravery comes not in a certain bloodline. But in the strength of one person's heart."

I couldn't drive the dagger home now, not in front of the princess. Because despite her wise words, she was not even a teenager. Even though she was born to rule, she did not need to see a cold-blooded death. I flipped Carp over and, using his own belt, tied his hands and feet together then rolled him into the tower.

Ash dragged the limp body of the other Ender in behind me. I noted that his opponent still breathed. We shared a look that said it all. There was enough trouble with how things had gone down in the Pit. We didn't need to double those issues by doing the same thing in the Deep. We stripped them of their weapons and barred the doors from the outside for an added measure, though I doubted the two guards would be going anywhere fast.

Finley pointed at the party. "Requiem is gone, I saw him leave. But he didn't take Belladonna with him; hurry." She bolted away, her billowy blue skirts dancing in the wind. I ran after her thinking I would catch up to her before she got to the crowd. She slipped between people and I was forced to shove my way in. Undine's pulled away from me, their eyes wide and I knew what they saw. An Terraling covered in blood and gore, her hair wild, weapons in her hands. Again.

"Get out of my way." I elbowed a woman too stunned to move and too wide to get around as fast as I wanted.

She fell to her butt and when she did, I stared at the scene in front of me. Belladonna was sitting on Requiem's lap. Her face was streaked with black, the kohl rimming her eyes having run with tears. Requiem didn't seem to care. Behind him hung a body, stripped of its flesh, green hair still attached, the twins huddling beneath it, their bodies shivering in what I could only assume was shock.

And Finley? She strode right up to Requiem, spun, and pointed at me. "I name Lark my champion, and you will face her, or be banished as is our creed."

Holy mother goddess, what had Finley done?

Chapter 19

Requiem tipped back his head and roared with laughter. "Finley, you are so damn feisty. At least we know our father's blood runs hot and true." He gave Belladonna's left breast a squeeze so hard his knuckles turned white, and her face paled. He looked straight at me as he did it.

Rage lit me up like a shooting star and I grabbed hold of my connection to the earth, letting it run through me.

Except I wasn't really seeing what he was doing. Didn't register the blue ticks of magic flowing up his hand until the wave caught me and pulled me into the central tank, once again. I went down, deep, felt something bump me. Knew what it was—one of Requiem's pets. If I never saw another shark again, it would be too damn soon.

My connection to the earth was still there, still humming along my synapses, and I wasn't about to let my fear take control.

If I could break down sandstone, break down glass, into finite components of earth then surely I could put the process into reverse. I swam to the surface as I pulled on the sand below us, forming it into a spear. I saw the dark torpedo shape swimming fast toward me and I flicked my hand, sending my sand spear straight up through it.

The shark's body exploded as the spear nearly cut it in half. I let the spear drop and reform as a second shark dove for the kill. Twice more I sliced the sharks until none were left. Or at least, none left alive.

I swam to the edge. The tank was smooth, impossible to get out of. Except it was made of sandstone too. I drove my fingers into the tank, expecting there to be some resistance.

It was like putting my hand into clay that formed up around my fingers. I climbed out of the water swiftly and onto the throne room floor. Calling the earth's power, I drew the sand up and hardened it over the water, sealing the edges. Finley grinned at me and waved. "You see, Requiem? She is my champion. Now, face her or be banished!"

Requiem all but flung Belladonna away from him and into Ash. He caught her and pulled her farther away. I caught his eye and he gave me a nod. I would be on my own for this fight. A challenge was a challenge. Requiem noticed none of that as he glared at Finley.

"This is not my first challenge, *wife*."

She tipped her tiny chin up. "I know. But it will be your last."

Oh, if only I had the confidence she did. Requiem stalked toward me. "When I kill you, I think I will have to kill my young bride too. I didn't realize how devious she was."

"You weren't the only one she outsmarted." I sidled to the left, over the covered tank. I only had the two daggers I'd started with, and the tiny thin dagger of Ash's tucked inside my vest. Finley had made the final bid for her throne, and it had put not only her life on the line, but mine, Ash's, and Belladonna's.

All or nothing, I had no choice but to kill Requiem.

"I'm disappointed, Lark," Requiem said softly, almost as if he were still trying to seduce me. "I thought you and I were going to get to know each other much better. Your sister, she's a grand champion in bed, but you with those long legs and Ender stamina . . . we could have had fun together."

I lunged forward, catching him off guard, sending him stumbling back over his own feet. "Enough talking. Fight or leave. Those are your choices."

Snarling, he came at me. At least I'd taken care of his familiars. He couldn't toss me back into the water and hope they would take me out. He no longer had that leg up on me. He stopped suddenly and backed away. "I will not fight you with weapons."

He lifted his hand and I saw the intent this time. I dropped to the ground as the wind surged around us, throwing people left and right. He was strong, but undisciplined. Untaught.

"Couldn't get anyone to show you the ropes without giving away you were a half-breed?" I yelled over the wind. The intensity of the gale picked up, people screamed and debris flew through the air. I focused on the power of the earth, letting it run through me and hold me to the ground. I hoped Ash was doing the same. Requiem had lots and lots of "oomph", but zero finesse.

I understood that problem far better than I liked to admit.

The wind died as suddenly as it had started and I rose slowly to my feet. Requiem glared at me as if it were my fault his little fit hadn't gone according to plan.

He ran at me, and I met him in the middle. So much for no weapons. Our blades clanged off one another, sending sparks into the night air. Behind him, I saw a flicker of gray and white dart across to the podium where the thrones sat.

Peta.

Requiem kicked out, catching me in the knee. My joint popped out and I screamed as I went down, the pain stunning me. It was only when I looked down at me knee that I understood why it was so bad. Requiem had spikes in the toe of his boots. Tiny shark teeth that were black to match.

"The poison will take you slowly, painfully," he crouched beside me as a spasm rocked my body. I arched, unable to stop the motion, which thrust my breasts up toward Requiem.

But he didn't touch me. "Your man, Ash. You weren't really fighting with him, were you? What a clever ruse to send him into the cells to find your ambassador. I must say, you would have been a far finer catch than Belladonna if you were anything but an Ender."

My teeth chattered hard, but I felt the poison dissipating already. Griffin's necklace was doing its job. But I forced my body to stay arched, to keep shaking.

To keep up the ruse.

"Nothing to say now, Princess?" He turned his head, his eyes going wide as a blur of white and gray bowled him over. I scrambled up, grabbed my dagger, and climbed his body as a snow leopard who could only be Peta's other form, held him down by the throat. Her canines drove in deep, tearing through the flesh. Blood spurted in great sprays, staining her coat.

I lowered my dagger. "And he shall be killed by the one who carries the tooth of the great cat." Blue had been wrong, it hadn't been a griffin tooth, but a leopard tooth she'd seen in her dream.

Requiem's eyes bugged as he stared at me, lifted his hands once, and a flicker of magic coursed along them. I softened the ground under him and pushed him down, encasing his hands in the sand that I quickly formed into glass. Rage lit his eyes, then left as his life bled out of him. His eyelids drooped closed and the breath eased out of him.

Peta gave him one last shake and then dropped him, spitting out his blood. "Filthy water brat." She glared at me, her intense green eyes narrowed to mere slits. "Don't think I did this to help you."

I held up my hands. "Never. But thank you, just the same. Is your master—"

"Killed. Not that he didn't deserve it. And now I must go back to the mother goddess and explain I've lost another of her children. . ." She shook her head, spotted coat rippling as she shifted into her smaller form. With a flick of her whit-tipped tail, she left me standing over Requiem's still warm body.

The world was silent only for a moment.

Finley raised her hands. "I declare this a day of independence. A day of freedom for all."

The crowd around us cheered, and for the first time they truly sounded happy. They hated Requiem, but they feared him more.

Finley stepped forward, and I bowed to her. She was no mere child. She was a queen in the making, and a damn tricky one too. "Your majesty, I believe the throne is yours."

She glanced at Belladonna who still sat with Ash, unseeing near the throne. "Your sister won't contest it?"

I shook my head. "I don't think that will be an issue."

Around us the crowd shifted into a wild dancing mob that lifted Finley above their heads. "Release my Enders from the cells at once!" she cried out. I watched her for a moment before going to my sister. Belladonna stared past me, her gray eyes clouded as if she saw things that weren't there. She was barely covered in a thin piece of turquoise material that was completely sheer. Requiem and his damn games.

I touched her hand, shocked at how cold her skin was despite the warmth of the air. "Bella, it's time to go home."

She blinked slowly, her fingers tightening around mine for a split second before flinging my hand away from her. Her mouth hardened. "Do not ever call me Bella again."

I stood, trying not to feel the hurt of her words, stepped back, and gave her a bow from my waist. "Ambassador. It is time to return to the Rim." Was this just a ruse for the Undines? Or had something happened while I'd been trying to get to her?

Belladonna stood and smoothed her hands over her dress. "I can't return home in this."

"Here . . ." Ash stepped beside me, holding out a thick piece of dark cloth that sparkled with silver bits woven into it. "Ambassador, will you allow me to help you with this?"

Her chin came up and she gave a slight nod. Ash wrapped it

around her body and then handed me the ends, I finished the job, wrapping her body in the silver colored material, tying it off at her hip.

Belladonna glanced down at my handy work. "Now take me home. Immediately."

We didn't argue with her. Ash led the way, cutting through the crowd. I walked behind Belladonna, my mind struggling with everything that had happened. Putting the pieces together of why and what were easy in some ways. Requiem had wanted to rule the Deep, but he'd also been laying the groundwork for a bloodline that would have ruled the entire world of elementals.

I thought about the ring Cassava had worn, how it had allowed her to control people by using Spirit. What would have happened if Requiem had gotten his hands on that? A full body shudder wracked me and I put my mind away from that. I'd hidden the ring myself in a place no one would look. A place that would remain hidden.

Still, the thought crossed my mind that if there was one ring, would there be another; maybe there really was one for each elemental family. The legends said there were, but . . . I stuttered to a stop as my mind latched onto the idea that maybe Requiem wasn't a half-breed. Maybe he'd had a ring like Cassava. "Wait."

Belladonna and Ash turned around to stare at me. She raised an eyebrow. "We are leaving."

I touched my armband. "Not without this, you aren't. Wait here, I have to check something." I bolted the way we'd come, weaving through the courtyard and back into the throne room. Most of the Undines had dispersed and those left were pointedly not looking at Requiem's body.

He hadn't been moved and lay face up, eyelids closed and blood over his chest and neck. I approached him carefully, hoping my hunch was wrong. Which was a funny thing because if he was a powerful half-breed, he should have been more frightening. Yet the idea of multiple rings that could control the elements terrified me. In the wrong hands, they would become weapons by which the wrong people could take power with ease.

Like Requiem.

Like Cassava.

I crouched by his body and lifted up his left hand. No rings. I scooped the right hand up, no rings there, either. A sigh of relief escaped me and I bowed my head.

"Lark," Belladonna said. "What are you looking for?"

She stood there and I stared up at her, at the stone hanging from her throat, the gray flecks within the smoky diamond that matched her eyes so well. I stood, unable to take my eyes from it. "Did Requiem . . . give you that?" I pointed at the necklace and her hand rose to it, fear lacing her eyes.

"No, I took it. It's the least I can have for . . . what happened." Defiance mingled with the fear, and I closed my eyes, searching for the right words.

I opened my eyes and held out my hand. "May I see it?"

Frowning, she slipped it off her neck and placed it in my hand. I clenched my fist around it and thought about a breeze that would wrap around my body. Maybe nothing would happen; I felt no different.

The warmth of the wind curled around me in a twist that tightened, pressing hard against my skin. I gasped and loosened my hold on the stone. "Take anything else, but you can't have this."

Belladonna's eyes widened then narrowed just as fast. "That stone is mine, Ender."

Ash shook his head at me. "Just let her have it, Lark. A stone like that can be found anywhere."

Worm shit, he didn't understand. "No."

A burst of laughter across the room, and they looked away from me. I raised my hand and twisted the armband, hoping with Requiem's death, the ban had been lifted.

The world swirled around me and I was sucked through to the Rim in the space of two heartbeats. Far easier when I wasn't submerged in someone else's memories. It was still dark in the Rim. The morning hadn't yet broken. The Traveling room was quiet and I bolted out of the barracks, headed for the hiding place I'd picked for Cassava's ring.

For now, I would put them together. But I would have to hide them again, maybe separately. No one stirred as I ran toward the planting fields. At the farthest end was the blighted field, and the large black rock that had been placed at the edge to warn people away.

Frantic, I dug like a madwoman, fear driving me. Down and under the big rock, in a tiny hollowed out miniature cave sat the pulsing, pink ring Cassava had always worn, the diamond glittering at me. I jammed the smoky gray diamond in beside it and covered them. Grabbing a downed tree branch I swept the area to cover the fact anyone had been digging.

Breathless, I ran back for the Ender's barracks, I had to get to the Traveling room and back to Ash and Belladonna. Into the barracks, my mind racing, I didn't stop to think; I just sprinted through the training room and back down the stairs.

I hit the Traveling room door and pushed it open. Pulling the globe with my hands, I saw the pale, anemic dirt of the blasted field under my nails. "Shit." If they were looking, they would see that, maybe even figure out where I hid the diamond that controlled the winds.

"Unless," I pulled the globe to me, bringing the Deep into sharp relief. I touched the place over the docks.

Right over the water.

A twist of the armband forward and I was sucked away from the Rim into the Deep. My feet were on the water for a split second before I plunged down. I swam to the shoreline, trying not to think about all the things waiting for me under the waves. All of Requiem's pets looking for revenge for their master's death. "Maybe not such a good idea." I swam as hard as I could, knowing the splashing would attract anything hunting.

Images of open jaws and razor sharp teeth chased me out of the water. I stood for a minute, daring myself to glance back. There was nothing in the pristine water, no dark shapes, no triangular fins. Yet I knew it would be a long time before the water felt safe to me again. If it ever did.

When I reached the throne room, Ash and Belladonna were standing, arguing, Finley beside them. She saw me first and smiled. I gave her a wave, fatigue washing through me. We were almost done.

"She will come back, Belladonna. Whatever she's doing is important." Ash had his fists on his waist.

Even at the distance I stood, the glare on Belladonna's face was visible. "She left us here, Ash."

I cleared my throat. "And I came back."

Her eyes would have shot arrows at me if she'd been capable, I was sure. "Give me my diamond."

Finley smiled. "If Lark wanted the diamond, then she may have it. She saved us all."

That wasn't exactly accurate since Peta had performed the killing blow. But I would take it if it meant Belladonna wouldn't contest me for the Sylph diamond. I should have known better.

The rage that lit up her face made her look so much like her mother that I took an involuntary step back.

"You will give me the diamond back. Give it to me!" Belladonna launched herself at me, her fists flailing through the air as tears tracked her cheeks. She bit my arm before I could catch her. Grunting, I pulled her off me and when Ash made a motion to help, I shook my head.

"Bella, what is going on? What happened?"

She slumped in my arms, huge sobs wracking her body. "I can't tell you, not with him here. He will tell me it is just. That the punishment is my reward."

Startled, I looked up at Ash. "Give us a few minutes."

"Let me know when you are ready to Travel." He bowed at the waist and strode away.

Holding her tightly, I sank to the floor with her. Belladonna's head rested on my shoulder as she cried herself out. "Lark, why did you take the diamond?"

I went with a half-truth. "It's dangerous, cursed. I didn't want it to hurt you so I . . . got rid of it."

"Oh. You were protecting me?" Her eyes softened. She wiped her face as she hiccupped back a sob.

I stroked her hair with one hand. "I've been trying to protect you the whole time. That hasn't changed."

"But you couldn't keep me safe from Requiem." Her words were barely above a whisper.

A growing horror filled me, and the words choked me. "Did he . . ." I'd hoped Requiem's words had been just to make me angry, to push me into making a mistake. That he hadn't actually done anything to her, that he hadn't had time.

She nodded and I clutched her too me. "I'm so sorry, Bella, I came as fast as I could."

"He raped me before the wedding. I thought . . . I thought I could tease him like I'd teased the others and get him to do what I wanted. But he didn't stop when I told him to." She paused, her eyes slowly lifting to mine. "Do you know what happened with Ash and me?"

Jaw tight, I nodded. Ash's memories were all too vivid within my head. "Yes. Cassava made you, didn't she?"

Belladonna sobbed. "Yes, and I like him, but not like that. It was awful, but now . . . now it's like this is my punishment. That's why I don't want Ash to know. He'd be happy that I've been hurt. The way he was."

I was shaking my head before she even finished. "Ash isn't like that. He is a good man."

Finley stepped forward, stopping our conversation, her eyes darting to Bella's stomach. "Belladonna, do you want to keep it? My healers can help you if you would like."

"How could you possibly know . . . that?" I whispered.

Finley gave me a sad smile. "It is part Undine. And as its queen, I can sense it."

Bella shook even harder and again the horror within me grew. The question was on the tip of my tongue but I couldn't even say it. Her eyes were clamped shut and she nodded. "My mother . . . she'll kill me if she finds out, even if I don't keep . . . What do I do?" She looked up at me, eyes awash with fear.

Holding her in one arm, I reached up and twisted the cedar band around my bicep. "We go home."

Chapter 20

Belladonna's memories on the way home were as bad as the first. Except it wasn't only one beating, but all of them rushing through her mind and into mine. One after the other, and for such silly things I struggled to comprehend.

Touching Mother's dress to feel the material.

Making eye contact when she wasn't supposed to.

Speaking.

Breathing.

Laughing.

We collapsed inside the Traveling room. Belladonna looked away from me. "You saw, didn't you?"

"I'm sorry. I don't know how to not see."

She sniffed and wiped her face. "Lark, I don't know what to do."

"Neither do I. But Father—"

"No. I can't trust him. I trust you, Lark. Tell me what to

do," she pleaded and I understood. Her whole life had been directed by Cassava. And now she wanted me to direct her the same way. I couldn't do it, though.

"What do you want?" I sat beside her, the globe swirling around us silently.

She fiddled with the hem of her skirt. "I don't know."

"Then for right now, I think you should wait. There is time yet . . . I think." Mother goddess help us both. I hoped I was giving her good advice. "I have to go back for Ash."

She caught my hand. "I never really liked him like that. Mother made me." Horror filled her eyes and she clamped her hands over her head. "Mother goddess, this is my punishment, isn't it?"

I hugged her to me. "Bella, that's not how life works. It isn't, I promise. Wait here, Ash and I will be right back." I stepped away from her, repositioned the globe with my fingers, and twisted the armband. The blessed quiet of Traveling without someone surrounded me and then I was back in the Deep. I stumbled as I stepped out of the ether, on the edge of the stairs that led into the throne room. I'd missed my target by a bit, but close was good enough for me.

"Third time's the charm," I said, thinking I was alone.

"Oh, I doubt that."

Requiem.

How was that possible? I'd seen him die!

I spun, unable to understand what was happening until the wave picked me up and slammed me against the wall. I slid down, the back of my head warm with a rush of blood. I saw his face, the puncture marks in his neck mostly healed, the glittering black of his eyes. His hands were torn up, but intact. He'd yanked them out of the glass boxes I'd put them in, tearing the skin down to bone in places.

"You think you can stop me? You fools; you didn't even check to make sure I was truly dead. That's what you get for depending on a familiar to do your job."

"How could you survive?" I couldn't stop the question from escaping me as I backed away.

He grinned. "You can draw on your familiars life force, and use it to boost your own. If you have a familiar that is."

Apparently I hadn't killed all his sharks.

He beckoned to me with both hands, fingertips lighting up with the blue of his magic, the build up of the ocean behind him visible. "Come to me, pretty Ender. I think Mako was right; I need to start bedding my women when they're dead."

I rushed toward him, as he wanted, the only thing in my hand the tiny knife Ash had given me. I caught Requiem by the arm as the massive wave rolled down, sweeping us both into the maelstrom of seawater. Tumbled about, I breathed easy, the hook still deeply embedded in my ear even if I could see nothing but flashes of light and dark.

Requiem grabbed a handful of my hair and yanked my head backward, his other hand mauling my face. I jerked my head away as his fingers traveled over my skin, searching.

A flash of understanding hit me.

He was looking for the hook, stealing my ability to breathe under water. Kicking and striking out, I knew it was only a matter of time before he went to my ear in his search. We wrestled and spun, our limbs tangling in a twisted mimicry of a gentler act. I finally booted him in the stomach, shoving him away from me.

The water around us stopped moving and the weight of it increased, like I'd been loaded down with sand in my pockets. Blinking rapidly, I stared at Requiem in front of me, already knowing what I'd see. But I was wrong. I could still breathe.

He held the griffin tooth necklace, a grin on his face. Blue must have told him that whoever wore the necklace would kill him. Damn her.

With a flick of his wrist he threw the griffin tooth away from him. Twisting and turning, it fell into the depths.

Requiem swam around me, and I turned with him. I had to believe that not having the necklace didn't mean I couldn't beat him.

The anger in me was fading, and I scrambled to grab a hold of it. The earth was not so far below us, and I reached out to it. Rocks shot up at my command, breaking apart, and shattering into shrapnel that sliced through the water and into his body. He jerked and danced, like a marionette, blood tainting the water.

His hands glowed blue. His plan was to drive the water into me. I remembered all too well the feeling of water being shoved into my eyes, nose, mouth, and ears from the mother goddess.

I wouldn't survive it, that much I knew.

Swimming away from him was a futile effort, but I tried anyway. Already the water pushed on my entire body, searching for a way in, forcing me to stop swimming in order to squeeze my legs together. I clamped my eyes and mouth shut and covered my ears with my hands. The water pressure increased, forcing its way into my nose. I gulped the water that flowed down the back of my throat, knowing it was only a matter of time.

As suddenly as the pressure started, it was gone. I opened my eyes, shocked at what I saw.

Peta swam around Requiem, pulling his attention to her as she swatted at him. The snow leopard did not look comfortable in the water in the least, but she was fighting for me.

Damn it, I did not want to like that cat.

I didn't waste the time she bought for me. I swam hard, cutting through the water. Reaching Requiem, I booted him in the stomach. He curled toward me, his eyes going to the side of my head, lighting up as he no doubt saw the earring.

He launched toward me and I tried to avoid him, but he snaked out a hand, clipping the side of my head and tearing off the hook in my ear.

With my air source gone, I had no choice but to end the fight now or die. Peta swam for the surface, and Requiem grabbed me, his thoughts flowing into my head as he twisted my hand, forcing me to drop the knife. His eyes widened, and then a slow grin spread over his face, showing every tooth he had.

You can hear me. I see it in you now. You are the one I seek. The child of Spirit.

There was only one thing left to do, the one thing that terrified me.

The part of me that was Spirit hovered just under my skin, beckoning to me. I had no choice; I had no other way to save myself.

I pulled Spirit tightly around me, delving into the power. Working completely on instinct, I pushed the command into my voice.

"Take me to the surface." The words were barely bubbles of air, but Requiem began to swim upward, the pressure on us gone.

We broke through the water and I gulped in a breath of air. We weren't that far from the Deep, maybe only a hundred feet from shore. Might as was well have been ten miles for all the difference it made to me.

Requiem yanked me closer to him, his arms going around me as his legs locked onto me. "Child of Spirit, you are one of the last, and I will make you mine to breed a new world of rulers under me. Not even Cassava would be as powerful as you and I together."

My arms and legs were held tightly, and I had lost my last weapon.

The desire to use Spirit to save myself rose up in me and I saw the pathway that I would take. Commanding Spirit, I could kill Requiem, would show my father I should be his heir. I would rule the Rim, have anyone I wanted at my side no matter who. My people would be forced to love and respect me.

I would be unstoppable.

It was as if a mirror were placed in front of me, seeing what I would become. My eyes narrowed with suspicion, my heart empty of love as I forced those around me to bow to me, twisting their minds to do as I wished.

I would become Cassava if I followed that path.

And I suddenly understood why my mother didn't save herself; the cost wasn't worth it, not for my own life. Everything I knew would be false if I used Spirit for my own devices. My soul would no longer be my own and that was a price I wasn't willing to pay. I relaxed. "Kill me then, for I will never bow to you."

A long, ruddy tentacle rose up behind him, and hanging from it dangled my necklace—griffin tooth dripping with seawater.

"No, I won't kill you. But I will make you wish I had." He leaned forward and bit me, his teeth driving into the muscles connecting my neck to my shoulder. I screamed, as much out of frustration as pain, then biting the sound off. I refused to let him have the pleasure of hearing me cry out.

Behind him the coiling tentacles reach forward. "I wouldn't be so sure," I whispered.

Olive's tentacles sliced out of the water, five of them scooping Requiem up, one on each arm and leg, and one wrapped around his neck. His face purpled and then went white with fear. "You will never stop her, Larkspur. I know her plans. I could help you," he screamed and I opened my mouth to tell Olive to wait. He could only mean one "her."

Cassava.

The giant squid flexed and Requiem's body flew apart, his head dropping into the water in chunks in front of me. As brutal as Olive had been with Requiem, she gently scooped me out of the water and ferried me back to dry land. Peta stood on the beach, shaking her—once again—tiny body.

"Thanks, Peta, you saved me again. But why did you come back?" I crouched so I could look her in the eye.

She grunted. "I stayed because you have no familiar and obviously are in need of help. As to the rest, perhaps the mother goddess will forgive me for Loam's death, if I tell her I saved your life—*twice*. She seems to have taken a shine to you."

I didn't know what to say. The housecat flicked her tail and stalked away from me.

A long, deep red tentacle flicked out of the water, and from it dangled Griffin's necklace. Olive lowered it so I could pluck it from her. I touched her gently as I slipped the necklace off. "Thank you, Olive."

Her head came up so I could see the strange eyes watching from under the water. Waving several of her arms at me, she slid back into the depths. I slid the necklace back on, the water dripping off it and down my chest. I let out a breath and the fatigue of the fight hit me square in the guts.

Hands caught me as I stumbled and Ash spoke softly. "The princess is fine." He helped me back to the throne room where the destruction was obvious. Finley was laid out on the floor, but her chest rose and fell evenly. Everything had been turned upside down and inside out with the tidal wave Requiem had used to wash us out to sea. Yet, beside Finley were my weapons I'd brought with me. Most importantly, my mother's spear. I bent down beside the princess—no, queen—and scooped up my armaments, slowly re-attaching them too me. I glanced at Ayu as she tended to Finley. "She'll be all right?"

"Yes, she will be fine. Thank you. You saved us all." Ayu said softly.

I nodded, unable to find any words for her. I hadn't really saved them, in the end, Olive had finished Requiem off, not me.

Ash's hold tightened on me. "Let's go home."

I reached to my armband and twisted it, sending us through the ether back to the Rim.

A recent memory of Ash's came forward.

"You care for her, don't you? That's the real reason you came to the Deep." Belladonna flipped her hair back as she eyed him up. The material Lark had wrapped around Belladonna covered her, and yet she clutched at herself as if she were freezing.

Ash stiffened as the words sunk into his brain. How had she known?

"My reasons are my own, Princess."

"Don't you hurt her," Belladonna hissed at him and he stared at her in surprise. "She is too good for you, too good for anyone I know, and I won't let you hurt her."

"Only a minute ago you were furious about her stealing the diamond, and now you would defend her?" He wasn't really angry, but he had never seen Belladonna, or any of Cassava's children for that matter, stand up for anyone else. Least of all their younger sister.

The memory was short and cut out as we dropped into the Traveling room. Belladonna sat on the floor, her head in her hands.

I didn't look at Ash, just went to her and helped her stand. "Come on, let's get you cleaned up and some real clothes on."

Anything to keep from looking at Ash and asking him why he had really come to the Deep.

Chapter 21

The next few hours were a blur of activity. Belladonna was sent to the healers first then Ash and I took our turns.

When I stepped out of the healers' rooms, I was shocked to see Dolph waiting for me. I couldn't stop myself. I threw my arms around him and hugged him. "I thought you were dead."

"Not quite," he grunted, patting me awkwardly on the shoulder. I wanted to ask him about Urchin, how he could kill his own son, if it was really necessary. But the new lines on his face, etched by sorrow and grief were testament enough. He made a motion with a rolled piece of paper, sealed with a deep blue wax crest of the Kraken that looked a great deal like Olive. "I've brought a message from our queen. Will you take me to your father?"

I nodded and led the way through the Spiral to our throne room. It hummed with activity, people coming and going,

Father making decisions on disputes. As if my life and the life of his eldest daughter had not only recently been in jeopardy.

I cleared my throat. "Your Highness, a messenger from the Deep."

My father looked up, surprised. "Ender Larkspur, you and the ambassador are back? I'm surprised."

A niggling fear wormed into me. What if he had wanted us dead, would he be trying to find a new way now to get rid of us?

Dolph stepped forward, bowed and straightened. He held a paper out, which he read from.

"By order of Queen Finley, first child of the Deep and ruler of the oceans, the Undines hereby thank King Basileus for his wisdom in sending Ender Larkspur and Ambassador Belladonna. Queen Finley would like to acknowledge that without the support of these two Terralings, her throne would still be held by an imposter." Dolph looked at me. "And you may call upon the queen should you ever have need, Larkspur." He clapped a hand on my shoulder. "Well done, Ender."

A flush of pride filled me with the words and I turned, expecting to see my father smiling.

He was not. In fact, he was frowning. "Ender Larkspur, to my private rooms. Now."

I knew what was coming. We were not supposed to interfere. Head held high, I strode toward the door on the side of the throne room that would take me to my father's private rooms.

The moss under my feet was no comfort as I waited.

He burst through the door, raging. "Of all the things I said, I told you not to interfere!"

"You told me to protect my sister at all costs; helping Finley was a part of that!"

"Blatantly disregarding my command, insolence on a scale I've never seen . . ."

The main door burst open and Belladonna burst in, hair and skirts flying behind her. "Don't you reprimand her, Father! Don't you dare. She kept me safe when any other Ender would have given up on me!"

He raised his free hand and pointed at her. "Belladonna, you are as much at fault as she is! I should banish you both."

"The other families already believe you are weak, how much worse will it be when you banish the two daughters the Undines are hailing as heroes," she said, her voice remarkably even for the flush of color in her cheeks.

Father's jaw twitched and for just a moment, I thought I saw the pink glow of Spirit around his eyes. But that was impossible, I'd buried the ring Cassava had, there was no way she could be controlling him still.

Which meant he was just being horrible all on his own.

He pointed at me, then Belladonna. "For now, you may stay."

I wasn't done, though. I steeled myself for what I was going to say and do. "We sent you a message. Did you get it?"

He nodded. "I did."

A tiny piece of my heart broke. "And were you going to send help?" Please, please let him say he would have.

Our father said nothing, only spun on his heel and walked out. Confusion rocked me. I didn't understand how he could go from one extreme to the other. It made sense when Cassava controlled him, but not now.

"It is the damage done to his soul, splitting it in the middle. The dark on one side, the light on the other."

The mother goddess's voice flowed into the room and Belladonna gasped. A glittering, glowing woman, her features indistinct but somehow still familiar, stepped through the wall, her body emerging from the tree before pulling away from it. Where her feet had walked, flowers erupted in every color I'd ever seen. I went to my knees and Bella did the same.

"Mother," I whispered.

She placed a hand on my head. "His heart is broken in pieces, and he does not know how to heal it, Lark. Your mother always did that for him, helped him hold Cassava's taint at bay. Now you must be the one to guide his heart until it is whole."

Her hand drifted from my head and went to Belladonna. "Child, the baby you carry will be the new life you need to find your place in this world. Love her as you wished to be loved." Bella sucked in a sharp breath and my eyes prickled with tears.

I reached over and took her hand. "I will stand with you, Bella. No matter what comes."

Her gray eyes filled with tears that trickled down her cheeks. "And I will stand with you, Larkspur. No matter what you face."

The room was empty, the mother goddess gone as quickly as she came.

I walked Bella back to her rooms. "We never asked him if he was trying to kill us."

She shrugged. "Does it matter? We know someone was, and that just means we have to be on guard."

Before I left her, I made sure she was okay. After our time together, I was reluctant to leave her on her own. "I'm worried you'll get into trouble," I said.

Laughing, she shook her head. "Not here, not at home."

After Dolph left to return to the Deep, I headed out of the Rim, jogging south. Looking for Griffin. As it was, he found me, long before I ever reached his home. A big black wolf with midnight black eyes waited for me at the top of a small ridge.

I held up the necklace. "Thank you. It saved my life."

He shifted into his human form, tall and broad, black haired with dark eyes. Handsome, I suppose, but his coloring made me think of Coal which only made my stomach hurt. "Yeah, it probably will again. Keep it."

Tucking it back into my vest I nodded. "I have a question for you, since you know the mother goddess maybe better than I do."

He snorted and reached for a long stalk of fern. "Viv can be a sassy wench. What did she do this time?"

Viv? The mother goddess had a name and Griffin knew it? Another time I would have to ask him about it. "She took away my ability to use the earth, and then when I wanted it back, made me swear my life to her."

His jaw dropped. "She didn't."

"She did. But I don't know what that means." I rolled my shoulders, fatigue and frustration vying for my attention.

Griffin let out a long low whistle. "Means a lot of things. One of which she can take your life away for no reason other than she chooses to. Or she could force you to do her dirty work, yeah?"

I blinked several times, not comprehending his words. "Dirty work?"

He froze, his nostrils flaring. "Later, we'll discuss it later. But be wary, yeah? She's got her hooks into you good now." In a flash, he shifted back to his wolf form and bolted away. The forest around us, though, was far from silent. I heard the footsteps and recognized the cadence. So, he'd followed me here. Interesting.

"I'm beginning to think he doesn't like me," Ash said.

I turned to face him. "Maybe you just smell bad. Maybe I should be upping your pedicure to a full day at the spa."

He laughed, reached out, and took my hand. A single tug and I was in his arms. "Enough talking with those lips. They have better things to do." He kissed me, his mouth sweet like the honey his eyes made me think of.

I dug my hands into his hair and held him tightly to me, his touch making my skin sing. I pulled back, and took a slow breath. "Where do we go from here?"

His eyes searched my face. "I don't know. Our lives will always be on the line; that is our job."

"And you can't always protect me," I said. "I am no longer a little girl needing to be watched over. I am not the heir to the throne. I am not a princess."

Ash didn't let go of me, and through our hands I could feel the tension rise in him. He glanced over his shoulder. "Things are about to get ugly, Lark. Whatever happens, just follow my lead."

Through the trees, four Enders ghosted toward us. Dressed in black leather with bright red hair topping each of them off, there was no doubt where they were from.

The Pit.

"Do we fight?" I tensed, reaching for my weapons.

"No. Your father has commanded us to go with them."

And suddenly I understood the kiss.

Ash was saying goodbye.

They surrounded us and it took everything I had in me to hold still, to allow them to stand behind me. My shoulder blades itched as though a knife blade were being held there, just a hairsbreadth from my skin.

Manacles were clamped over my wrists as my arms were jerked behind me. I was spun around to face a very familiar face. Red flaming curls and orange eyes glittering with barely suppressed hatred.

I gave her a tight smile. "Hello, Magma."

"Ender Larkspur, you are to be tried for the murder of three Enders hailing from the Pit." She yanked me forward forcing me to stumble. A steady calm flowed over me.

I looked at Ash, his hands behind him in manacles too. "Looks like your pedicure will have to wait. I think we're going back to finish what we started."

Whoever was trying to kill me from the Rim was going to have to get in line, because Fiametta was about to get her shot at me first.

COMING SOON

COMING FALL 2015

FIRESTORM
(THE ELEMENTAL SERIES, BOOK 2)

Authors Note

Thanks for reading "Breakwater". I truly hope you enjoyed the continuation of Lark and her family's story, and the world I've created for them. If you loved this book, one of the best things you can do is leave a review for it. Amazon.com is where I sell the majority of my work, so if I can only ask for one place for reviews that would be it it – but feel free to spread the word on all retailers.

Again, thank you for coming on this ride with me, I hope we'll take many more together. The rest of the Celtic Legacy, along with my other novels, are available in both ebook and paperback format on all major retailers. You will find purchase links on my website at www.shannonmayer.com. Enjoy!

About the Author

Shannon Mayer lives in the southwestern tip of Canada with her husband, dog, cats, horse, and cows. When not writing she spends her time staring at immense amounts of rain, herding old people (similar to herding cats) and attempting to stay out of trouble. Especially that last is difficult for her.

She is the *USA Today* Bestselling author of the The Rylee Adamson Novels, The Elemental Series, The Nevermore Trilogy, A Celtic Legacy series and several contemporary romances. Please visit her website for more information on her novels.

http://www.shannonmayer.com/

Ms. Mayer's books can be found at these retailers:

Amazon	iTunes
Barnes & Noble	Smashwords
Kobo	Google Play

Printed in Great Britain
by Amazon